D1050052

Irrepressible
SPIRIT

Irrepressible SPIRIT

Conversations With Human Rights Activists

SUSAN KUKLIN

G. P. PUTNAM'S SONS   NEW YORK

Photograph credits

The portraits of the participants in this book are by the author.
Other photographs have been provided by the following:
Doug Magee: page 117
The family of Chanrithy Ouk: page 164
Human Rights Watch: page 67
Jemera Rone: page 85
Usreel Pinto and Nando Neves of Imagenes de Terra: page 95
UPI: page 30

Library of Congress Cataloging-in-Publication Data
Kuklin, Susan.   Irrepressible spirit / Susan Kuklin.   p.   cm.
Includes bibliographical references.
Summary: Narrates personal testimonies of men and women who have experienced human rights
abuses and presents accounts of human rights workers and of Human Rights Watch.
1. Human rights—Juvenile literature. 2. Human Rights Watch (Organization)—Juvenile literature.
3. Human rights workers—Juvenile literature. [1. Human rights. 2. Human Rights Watch
(Organization) 3. Human rights workers.] I. Title.
JC571.K854 1996   323—dc20   95-41412 CIP AC
ISBN 0-399-22762-8 (hard cover)
10   9   8   7   6   5   4   3   2   1
ISBN 0-399-23045-9 (paperback)
10   9   8   7   6   5   4   3   2   1
First impression

Dedicated to
Bao Tong, his family,
and all the other political prisoners who dare
to speak out for justice and freedom.
May they return home safely and speedily.

Contents

Where, after all, do universal human rights begin? In small places, close to home—so close and so small that they cannot be seen on any maps of the world.

Eleanor Roosevelt

A Message from Robert L. Bernstein

*Book Publisher and Founding Chair
of Human Rights Watch*

Václav Havel, the writer and president of the Czech Republic, once said, "Each and every one of us can come to realize that he or she, no matter how insignificant or helpless he may feel, is in a position to change the world. We all have to start with ourselves. If we wait for someone else, none of us will ever see change. . . . Whoever applies it, may achieve something. If he does not even try, it is quite certain he will achieve nothing."

People often ask me how I became involved in human rights work. I didn't choose to become active. As a book publisher I was simply trying to support a few writers in the Soviet Union who were being treated unfairly. That was my first step.

One step led to another and to another. I found myself traveling a path that more often than not seemed overwhelming. In spite of that I realized that human rights work did more for me than I did for it. It made me feel alive. It broadened my interests in other parts of the world. And it put me in contact with thinkers of every kind.

Through the years I've come to see that the men and women who are attracted to human rights efforts are extraordinary individuals. By their brave work, they show how important it is for people in free countries to interact with human rights activists living under threat. If the world is to function with few wars and conflicts, the peoples in each part of the world must be able to govern themselves. I believe that people cannot govern themselves unless they are free.

There are many different ways to attack abuses and force change. A first step is to know what's happening in the world. A second is to understand what your own government is doing about what you know is happening. A third step is to write to your government—the President, your members of congress. It does have an effect. And a fourth step is to support a human rights organization.

To me upholding human rights is the single most important idea on the world political scene today. It is my hope that reading this book is your first step toward identifying yourselves as human rights activists who can transform the world.

Introduction

We the Peoples of the United Nations Determined

• to save succeeding generations from the scourge of war, which twice in our lifetime has brought untold sorrow to mankind, and

• to reaffirm faith in fundamental human rights, in the dignity and worth of the human person, in the equal rights of men and women and of nations large and small, and

• to establish conditions under which justice and respect for the obligations arising from treaties and other sources of international law can be maintained, and

• to promote social progress and better standards of life in larger freedom . . .

United Nations Charter (1945) (Preamble)
signed at San Francisco, 26 June 1945.
Entered into force on 24 October 1945.

About fifty years have elapsed since the United Nations developed its charter. Are we, the peoples of the world, living up to the noble ideals stated in this preamble?

Before answering this question, let us ask the men and women throughout the world who languish in prisons because they dared to criticize their governments. Ask the children who are separated from their parents and forced into camps, prisons, and brothels. And ask the families whose homes are destroyed and whose loved ones are murdered, raped, and tortured. Too often we have become violent, estranged peoples.

There is much evil in this world of ours, evil so appalling it boggles the mind. Hannah Arendt, the noted author and political theoretician who wrote about the nature of evil, described how acts of conscience or goodness can disappear into "holes of oblivion."

How do we guard against these holes of oblivion? How do we protect ourselves and others from evil? How do we ensure the human rights of all peoples? And what is a human right anyway?

A human right is something no one can take away from you. In other words it is something that is intrinsically yours. The right to live, the right to free speech, the right to practice the religion of one's choice, and the right to equality before the law are a few human rights. Theoretically, human rights are protected by international laws and treaties. All too frequently, these laws are violated, exploited, or simply ignored.

Sensational newspaper headlines, the rivers of nameless, wretched people seen on nightly news programs, and the unending statistics of murdered, displaced, or "missing" persons often have a numbing effect on us. But we must not allow ourselves to be indifferent to these horrors.

This book attempts to give a face to the faceless. In some of the testimonies, individuals give personal witness to human rights abuses they have experienced. Other testimonies center on the gathering and reporting of abuses. Researchers from a human rights organization, local monitors from assorted countries, student activists, and victims of abuse talk about their lives and experiences.

Although the people who participated in this book are from different backgrounds and diverse cultures, they have much in common. They speak out, often at great personal risk, so that we do not stand by silently while human rights abuses are taking place.

Although Hannah Arendt wrote about the holes of oblivion, she later came to a conclusion contrary to her earlier view. As reported in a review in *The New Yorker* magazine of the book *The Letters of Hannah Arendt and Mary McCarthy,* edited by Carol Brightman, Arendt said that "the resistance of even one man provides a moral and philosophical counterweight to the machinery of annihilation. . . . Experience has shown that there will always be some people who do not comply with terror, always one man who lives to tell the story. 'The holes of oblivion do not exist.' "

It is an honor and a privilege to bring to you a group of brave women and men who "do not comply with terror." They are but a few of the many who attempt to keep the human spirit from disappearing into the holes of oblivion.

ABOUT HUMAN RIGHTS
AND HUMAN RIGHTS WATCH

After World War II, the Nuremburg Tribunal, an international trial of twenty-four Nazi war criminals, introduced the idea that some crimes are of "such an egregious nature as to warrant judgment and punishment by international tribunals." A series of declarations was developed to set international standards for human rights. On December 10, 1948, the General Assembly of the United Nations adopted the Universal Declaration of Human Rights. Numerous regional and international agreements followed, including the Convention on the Prevention and Punishment of the Crime of Genocide (1948); the American Declaration of the Rights and Duties of Man (1948); the Helsinki Accords (1975); the International Covenant on Civil and Political Rights (1976); the African Charter on Human Rights (1978); the Convention Against Torture and Other Cruel, Inhuman or Degrading Treatment or Punishment (1987); and the Convention on the Rights of the Child (1989).

Governments sign treaties, and governments also break treaties. Some leaders raise their hands and pledge to guard and protect the rights of their people. Other leaders raise their hands to give orders that brutalize their people.

International and regional conferences have developed procedures to guard against gross human rights violations. Though they do not always admit to it publicly, most governments, especially those who depend on international trade and on tourism, concede that their international reputations greatly depend on their respect for human rights.

In 1975 the Helsinki Accords pledged to respect human rights, including "freedom of thought, conscience, religion, or belief." These accords were signed by the United States, Canada, the former Soviet Union, and thirty-two European countries.

After the signing, the Moscow Helsinki Group was formed under the leadership of physicist Yuri Orlov, Aleksandr Ginzburg, Anatoly Marchenko, Elena Bonner, Anatoly Shcharansky, and others to monitor human rights abuses in the Soviet Union. When the members of the group reported that human rights violations were taking place in their country, they were imprisoned or sent into exile.

Helsinki Watch, the forerunner of Human Rights Watch, was founded in the United States in 1978 by Robert Bernstein, Orville Schell, Aryeh Neier, Adrian DeWind, and Jeri Laber as a response to the imprisonment of the members of the Moscow Helsinki Group.

Three years later, when Ronald Reagan was elected president, intense debates raged over U.S. aid to the Contras in Nicaragua, and to Guatemala, Chile, and El Salvador. Americas Watch was founded because of concern for human rights violations in this hemisphere. The Watch grew and grew: Asia Watch in 1985, Africa Watch in 1988, Middle East Watch in 1989. Today, Human Rights Watch has grown into five divisions—Africa, the Americas, Asia, the Middle East, and the signatories of the Helsinki Accords—along with projects on Arms, Free Expression, Prisoners' Rights, Women's Rights, and Children's Rights.

As of this writing, the organization conducts investigations of human rights abuses in close to seventy countries around the world. It addresses the human rights practices of governments of all political stripes, of all geopolitical alignments, and of all ethnic and religious persuasions. Human Rights Watch documents violations by both governments and rebel groups during internal wars. The organization defends freedom of thought and expression, due process, and equal protection of the law; it documents and denounces murders, disappearances, torture, arbitrary imprisonment, exile, censorship, and other abuses of internationally recognized human rights.

Human Rights Watch works hand in hand with local human rights monitors. These smaller, domestic organizations have far less protection than the large, highly visible transnational Watch. Domestic monitors have been abducted, tortured, arrested, and murdered. And yet more and more people continue to speak out against human rights abuses. Irrepressible spirits all.

How I Wrote This Book

Writing a book about human rights feels like building a sky-scraper that becomes so high it blocks out the sky. I began by looking into the work of nongovernmental organizations that deal with nitty-gritty rights abuses. Although there are many abuses going on in the world, there are also many organizations of people who are ready, willing, and able to expose them: Amnesty International, the Lawyers Committee for Human Rights, Doctors Without Borders, and Human Rights Watch, to name a few.

Networking was my first step. My friend Susan Herman, a professor at Brooklyn Law School and a board member of the ACLU, suggested that I speak with Gara LaMarche, the associate director of Human Rights Watch and the director of the organization's program on free expression.

At our first meeting, we talked about human rights in general and Human Rights Watch in particular. I returned home with a huge pile of the organization's articles, press releases, memos, and books about human rights violations throughout the world. The foundation of my skyscraper was now in place.

Gara then introduced me to Susan Osnos, the director of communications. We, too, had a long talk, and she gave me the names of people to speak with, along with more publications, memos, and press releases. Gara and Susan suggested I talk with Lois Whitman, who was just starting a new division: Children's Rights. Our conversation ended with Lois giving me articles, prepublication books, and materials on human rights violations of children throughout the world.

By this time my studio was piled high with materials. It was overwhelming. And the worst part of it was that the abuses were never ending.

I began attending Wednesday-morning staff, board, and advisory committee meetings of Human Rights Watch on a regular basis. At these heavily attended sessions, everyone received a packet of worldwide newspaper clippings that reported human rights violations. The stacks were thick.

Meetings were divided into two sections. Two researchers reported on two separate areas where specific abuses had taken place. These first-rate reports were carefully documented, introduced, and described. Researchers were insightful, respectful, and full of enthusiasm. Kenneth Roth, the executive director of Human Rights Watch, usually led the meetings. He impressed me with his unflinching resolve when it came to human rights. It did not matter whether the abuses originated in distant lands or here in the United States. These meetings were off the record and simply provided me with an understanding of the organization.

Each year, Human Rights Watch honors local monitors from countries around the world. At the 1994 event, I spent five days with these monitors. During a day-long retreat, the Watch monitors asked the local monitors how they could best be served. The answers were fascinating. The camaraderie was life affirming.

More, more, more materials. As time went by, the many issues of abuse threatened to topple my skyscraper. It became necessary to pare down the material.

I forget how I met Li Lu, whose story appears in Chapter 1, but I feel as if I have known him since 1989, when he appeared on my TV screen during the Tiananmen Square student movement. (A major reason why I wanted to write this book was what happened at Tiananmen.) Li Lu gave my skyscraper a new direction when he introduced me to the terrific folks at the Reebok Human Rights Foundation, an organization whose sole (no pun intended) purpose is to honor individuals under thirty who have made significant contributions to the cause of human rights. Through Reebok I met David Moya, who, along with Li Lu, was a recipient of their award.

Interviewing

Many of the people in this book are seasoned activists who are comfortable talking about their experiences. Some, however, have had fewer opportunities to talk publicly about their lives. On occasion, survivors made and canceled appointments. Interviews were often filled with tears, irony, and even laughter. Interviews were conducted mostly in English, but when necessary, interpreters from Human Rights Watch pitched in.

Secondary Materials

Human Rights Watch gave me unlimited access to their research and reports. Sometimes, when it was impossible for me to go into the field, I used their interviews to supplement my own. These are identified in the text.

In order to place issues in recent historical or legal context, I have included some political background, history, or law.

Prior to 1994, Human Rights Watch referred to its divisions as separate "Watches," e.g., Americas Watch, Asia Watch, etc.

After 1994, the organization renamed its divisions in the following manner: Human Rights Watch/Americas, Human Rights Watch/Asia, etc. For references and quotes, I have followed the organization's documentation guidelines existing at the time.

INTENTIONS

It is not my intention to point a finger at any one particular country or political ideology. Countries from every continent (with the exception of Australia and Antarctica) are included, but no single country is prominently featured more than once.

Although an argument can be made that all human rights abuses are political, I have not included those abuses that come about because of cultural or religious practices. I have included only a small sample of the many abuses inflicted on women and children all over the world.

Space limitations prevented me from reporting other important abuses, such as those against gay people, the use of child soldiers and child labor, or the disappearances or murders of civilians or activists.

ACKNOWLEDGMENTS

First and foremost, I would like to thank all the monitors and activists who participated in this book. I would also like to thank the entire staff of Human Rights Watch for inviting me into their lives and making me a part of their international family, including Robert L. Bernstein (chair), Kenneth Roth (executive director), Holly J. Burkhalter, Gara LaMarche, Alice

Brown, Susan Osnos, Maria Pinto Kaufman, Dorothy Thomas, Jemera Rone, Jeri Laber, Holly Cartner, Lois Whitman, Janet Fleishman, Florence E. Teicher, Robert Kimzey, and Derrick Wong. Special thanks to Alice H. Henkin for reading the manuscript.

There are many other individuals and organizations that helped make this book possible: the Reebok Human Rights Foundation, especially Sharon Cohen (executive director), Douglas Cahn, and Paula Van Gelder; Ruthellen Weiner and Eric Nadelstern at the International High School in Long Island City, New York; Stevan Weine, M.D., codirector of the Project on Genocide, Psychiatry and Witnessing, University of Illinois at Chicago; Professors Susan Herman, Ursula Bentele, Lan Cao, and Sam Murumba of Brooklyn Law School; and my editor, Refna Wilkin, and the wonderful art department at G. P. Putnam's Sons.

I have come to think of *Irrepressible Spirit* as a book about a family, the family of humankind. In keeping with this theme, I would like to take this opportunity to publicly thank mine. They taught me that those who *have* must care for those who *have not*. They taught me that no one is free unless everyone is free.

I also would like to express my gratitude to my husband, Bailey, who listened, challenged, proposed hypotheses, and probed my responses.

I

The Right to Freedom of Expression

Everyone has the right to freedom of opinion and expression; this right includes freedom to hold opinions without interference and to seek, receive and impart information and ideas through any media and regardless of frontiers.

Universal Declaration
of Human Rights
Article 19

CHAPTER 1

An Impatient Generation

Li Lu

Activist—China

During the 1989 student demonstrations in China, I tasted the dream of freedom. I only glimpsed it, but what I saw was so beautiful and so powerful that it won't easily leave my mind and my heart.

BAD ELEMENTS OF SOCIETY

My paternal grandparents were very influential at one time. My grandmother was one of the first women educated in China. In the forties, she was elected senator on the Independent ticket. When Mao and the Communists took power, my grandmother thought there wouldn't be much change. She didn't leave China as many of her friends did.

There were several political campaigns that targeted intellectual and business elites of the past. These people were called "bad elements of society." My grandmother was one of those, and she found herself in particular trouble because she was independent and educated. Labeled an "historic counter-revolutionary," she was put in prison in 1950.

My grandfather was a philosopher and social activist. He got his Ph.D. from Columbia University in the States and taught briefly at the University of Chicago. He was a very stubborn intellectual and apparently an able activist. When my grandfather lived in China, he was in trouble with Chiang Kai-shek. [Chiang Kai-shek, the leader of the Nationalist Party, was president of China in 1929–31 and 1943–49. His government, overthrown in a civil war led by Mao Zedong, moved to Taiwan.] When he lived in the States, he was blacklisted during the intolerant McCarthy era.

My grandfather believed that the Communist revolution might bring new hope for China. Chairman Mao was like a god figure. Nobody had any doubts about him. He was always right and all-powerful. Mao promised a coalition government. He promised elections. He promised a democracy. He promised to revitalize our economy and establish China as a strong country. These words and promises were really dear to my grandfather, who believed that a healthy society must be based on a system that protects an individual's rights. These ideas got him into trouble when he returned to China.

In 1957, close to a million, or by some estimates a million and a half, intellectuals were labeled "rightists" and sent into prisons and labor camps. One of the most famous rightists at the time was my grandfather. He died in prison ten years later.

My father, his son, had been selected by the Communists as one of 150 young people who were their most promising stars. These darlings of the country were sent to Moscow to study. Throughout the fifties and early sixties, my father remained in Moscow, where he was working on his Ph.D. in engineering.

By the time my father returned to China, his parents had already been sent to labor camps. He lived in Beijing and worked on a nuclear project. Like all the young people in China at that time, my father was completely in agreement with Mao. After a while he began to have suspicions that Mao, like the Soviet leader Stalin, was becoming a dictator. He began to compare Mao to Stalin publicly. Following the family tradition, he got into trouble. The Central Committee decided that he couldn't be trusted. He was sent to Tangshan, an industrial city southeast of Beijing.

I was born in Tangshan a few weeks before the start of the Cultural Revolution. That wasn't quite a pleasant time to be born. My father said that I must have known something bad was about to happen because I delayed my birth by almost a month. I just didn't want to come out.

About the Cultural Revolution

In 1966, in an attempt to "purify" Chinese communism and maintain strict control of the country, Chairman Mao Zedong directed a major crusade against the upper middle class.

This campaign included violent actions by a group of radical students known as the Red Guards. With the support of Mao's wife, Jiang Qing (a member of the then-powerful "Gang of Four"), artists, academics, and bureaucrats were imprisoned or publicly humiliated at "struggle meetings." Many leading citizens were forced to work as laborers. Universities were closed. About half a million people were killed.

The revolution was officially ended in 1969, but many of its tactics continued until 1976. After Mao's death, the Red Guards were disbanded and Jiang Qing and her Gang of Four were removed from power. A more moderate leader, Deng Xiaoping, himself a political victim imprisoned during the Cultural Revolution, became the chairman of the Communist Party.

Once the Cultural Revolution started, party leaders decided who were the bad elements or class enemies. My mother came from a very rich landlord family, and that was enough to get her into trouble. Soon after my birth, my parents were sent to work in the coal mines.

Since my parents could not take me with them, I was put in the care of a peasant family. I stayed with the family very briefly, and then they passed me along to another peasant family. Then another. Then another. I don't know why the peasant families didn't want me. Perhaps I wasn't a good baby. Or perhaps they were afraid they would get into political trouble if the authorities found out who that baby was. Everything was tightly controlled. Every new person had to be registered with village leaders and local police. Finally, when no one would take care of me, I was put into a child-care center.

LIZARD

My first recollections probably go back to the time when I was in the child-care center. For me it was an orphanage because I didn't have a family to go home to on weekends as did the other children. I was four years old. My earliest memories are of darkness, loneliness, and being bullied by everybody. I had to spend time alone during weekends, when everybody else was home with their family. But I always knew that I had parents because the teachers and other children alluded to them as the "bad people" or "counterrevolutionaries." That made me feel worse.

But I also made my first turnaround at the child-care center. I fought my way up from the bottom of the group to become the so-called first official. (The students created a hierarchy: first official, second official, and the kids at the very bottom.) We established our places by fighting. The determining factor of the fight was whether the person had self-confidence. If you were confident, you won. And if you won, you got into a high position. Then, when the grown-ups were not around, you could bully the kids below. Because I had the lowest confidence, I was at the bottom. I was made to think that I was nothing. But there was one incident that changed my life.

Our housing was not in good condition, so we had lots of lizards in the house and in the playground. All the children shared a fear of lizards. We believed that they were the most fearful, poisonous things, and treated them like semidevils. We believed that if a lizard touched you, the part that it touched would fall off. And if it touched your heart, you would die. That was the legend.

We all slept in a forty-bed room. After the teacher checked us and turned off the lights, we usually started a game by calling, "The lizard has gone into the coat of somebody-somebody." And that child would cry while everybody else laughed and shouted, "Yes." We never actually put the lizard in the coat, it was just a game. Calling out was intimidating enough to make you very fearful.

One night we chose a child who cried very easily. He cried so loud, the teacher came back to our room. He asked who had started this game, and the others accused me. "Dry Shrimp Eye started it!" That's what they called me, Dry Shrimp Eye *(sham ee a)*.

As punishment, the teacher ordered me to stand barefoot on the cold cement ground. As soon as he left, everybody began to call out and pretend that the lizard had gone to my bare feet. When I looked down at my feet, there was in fact a real lizard crawling very slowly over my feet. I was just horrified. I became numb.

After a while the teacher returned and ordered me back to my bed. I couldn't move and I couldn't speak. I was completely dominated by fear. The teacher put me to bed. For the whole night I dreamt about all kinds of terrible things. I dreamed that I became very big and parts of my body split off in different places: the leg, the hand, the head. It was just horrible.

The next day when I woke up, I didn't know where I was. Maybe I'm in hell, whatever that was. And I still couldn't move. Finally, I slowly lifted the quilt and looked at my feet. To my great surprise, they were still there. When I tried to move them, they responded to my order. It was a tremendous discovery to me. For several days I was completely amazed by this phenomenon. I did nothing but think about it again, again, again.

I came to the conclusion that somehow the lizard liked me. I figured the reason was that I was the only one who kept the lizards company when everybody else left for home. We shared a darkness and a loneliness, and so they had chosen me as a friend.

I began to test whether this was true. I let a lizard walk across my hand to see what would happen. Nothing happened. The next time I heard the other kids cry that a lizard had come into somebody-somebody's coat, I laughed quietly and said to myself, "This is your game, it's not my game anymore."

I began to develop a strange confidence, as if I was the only powerful person who could be with the lizards. Earlier, I was always worried about the first official, whom we called "White Face" when he wasn't around. ("White Face" means that you have good nutrition and are well taken care of. In the Peking Opera, the White Face is a standard character, somebody who is not a good person, who takes advantage of others.) Everybody was afraid of White Face, especially me.

I decided to have my revenge. One day I collected a lot of lizards and quietly put them into his quilt. When we were going to bed, I shouted, "The lizard has gone into White Face's quilt!" Everybody was shocked.

The others couldn't believe that a lizard would go to the first official's quilt. He opened his quilt and saw dozens of lizards crawling in different directions. He screamed. He cried. He couldn't control himself. When the teacher came to ask what happened, he couldn't say anything, and nobody else could say anything because they were completely shocked. I was the only one who slept very well that night.

For many days thereafter, the first official's face became whiter and whiter. Everybody thought that was the work of the lizards, even though he hadn't touched them, he had just opened the quilt.

Afterward, White Face decided on revenge. He remembered that it was I who had called out. He and his lieutenant tried to trap me. I ran to the corner of the yard and opened the bricks, and a lot of lizards came out. I got a few on my hands and feet. The others were so fearful. They thought that I was like a god because I was able to play with the lizards. Before White Face could hit me, I made the first move and struck him to the ground. Then I became the first official and got a new nickname, Lizard. And I was very famous.

EARTHQUAKE

I stayed in the child-care center for three years. From there I was taken in by a coal miner's family. The coal miner was the foreman who had taught my father how to become a miner. I don't know about their relationship, but to this day, my father has a high regard for him. He must have had a high regard for my father, too, despite the fact that my father was considered a "bad element," an independent intellectual who questioned the authority of Mao.

It was in the coal miner's home that I had a stable family life. I was about seven at that time. I stayed with them until I was ten. Even though the family had five children of their own, they treated me as a son. I regarded them as my only family for a long time, even after I left them.

24

At ten I was reunited with my real family. By now I had become a very strong boy, doing everything myself. I knew where to find food and water. I didn't need my parents. But also I realized that there was something missing in me. I knew that I was different from other children. I wasn't happy.

I became a wild street boy and fought all the time. It was compulsory to have an elementary education, so I went to school, but I was never a very good student. People thought that I was worthless. They spit on me because I came from a bad family background. I was the target of bullying. I was terribly depressed.

On July 28, 1976, one of the most devastating earthquakes on record destroyed Tangshan. Two hundred forty thousand people died, according to the official figure. There were lots of predictions about the earthquake, but nobody cared enough to warn us. Mao was dying, and the entire government was engaged in internal politics. Nobody cared about people in Tangshan. Afterward, there was no support. No medicine. No water. No food. We were powerless, helpless, voiceless. We were nobodies, nowhere. And yet we were real people.

Miraculously, although my own family's home collapsed, we were among the few who survived. Somebody dies and somebody lives. Everyone in the coal miner's family died. I was devastated. Why did I live? Why did they die? I was at a complete loss.

The earthquake became a symbolic event that ended an era. About a month later, Mao Zedong died. A month after that, a coup took place and the so-called Gang of Four, which included Mao's wife, Jiang Qing, were sent to prison. The Cultural Revolution was officially ended, and Deng Xiaoping came to power.

Deng brought about revolutionary change, without which I could never have done what I did through my college years and the events of Tiananmen Square. Society became more permissive. People vowed that what happened during the Cultural Revolution would never happen again.

My grandmother, finally released from prison, moved in with us. She was the only person who thought that I had a future. Once she said something that really touched me: "Well, the truth is that you fight all the time and that's not a nice thing to do. But you always fight against people who are stronger than you, you never fight a boy weaker than you. That means that you have a sense of the just." Justice. I never forgot that word. It was the first time anyone thought that I was good. She also said, "People can do different things in their lives. Some people help one person at one time. Some people help a lot of people most of the time. What distinguishes one from the other is education." That's a widely held Confucian belief, but coming from her, it took on a stronger meaning. She told me that with education, everything is possible. That was my beginning.

I began to get serious and started studying. I was eleven years old. Before that, I had never spent any minutes studying. That year I went on to become top of my class. I discovered that I didn't have to spend a lot of time studying in order to do well. I spent most of my time reading other things. Once I began junior high school, I went to boarding school because I was never quite happy with my own family.

All the books at the school had been rescued from the library after the earthquake, and they were totally unorganized. The books were left in a large room, and one woman who had lost her leg in the earthquake was assigned to take care of them. I happened to sit next to this lady's sister in class, and she asked if I would help her. I was completely lonely at that time. The books became tremendous friends. They helped me discover a new world.

From books, novels especially, I got a sense of the normal. Human relationships. But that didn't eliminate my sense of loneliness and of coming from nowhere. Suddenly I began to ask myself, Why don't I have a normal life? Who am I? Where did I come from? Who are my parents and grandparents? Who were those people who took care of me? And what was I going to do with my life?

My examination scores entitled me to go to the best senior high school. My parents were very happy about that. As a reward, they gave me money to spend the summer in Beijing. It was my first glimpse of a big city.

In Beijing, I found my grandfather's prison guard. The guard said, "The only thing I remember is there was a man who exercised regularly, even after he was interrogated. He always said that he was competing with Chairman Mao to see who would live longer." My grandfather died when Mao's reputation was at its apex. Everybody thought he was a madman.

When I found some of his unpublished writings, I was absolutely fascinated. He talked about philosophical ideas, the history of philosophy. In that repressive environment, when it was dangerous to think that the world could be different, he remained a liberal philosopher. I was able to find a spiritual companionship with my grandfather. I realized that somebody who was intimately, physically related to me had similar thoughts. I came away with the feeling that we thought as one.

But because he had paid a huge price, that was not entirely an easy feeling.

In high school, I reached out to more people. I became a student activist. I tried out my ideas on people to see whether there were others who felt as I did. I also wanted to overcome my sense of aloneness and helplessness. I had a lot of success in doing that.

I went to Nanjing University and majored in physics and economics. I became very active in student organizations. This gave me some confidence, some hope that we might be able to do something different.

More and more people were thinking about democracy. The lifestyle of people in America and Europe that we saw in movies was very attractive. There was a social momentum that called for bigger changes than Deng and the reformers wanted. Also, we were an impatient generation, determined to do things differently. We hoped that if others felt the same, we could dare to be counted.

At the end of 1986 and the beginning of 1987 there was a national student movement. At Nanjing University five of us began to organize a demonstration. A committee of five people against the government and policies of Deng Xiaoping. We realized it was entirely possible that no one would join our protest. The students did show up, but they got scared and returned to the university. Some of the other activists were expelled, and nothing was accomplished.

Then, in 1989, a new opportunity arose. There was one guy [Hu Yasbang] in the Communist Party who was the first official to advocate political change. As a result, he was expelled from his post. On April 15 he died. We felt that everybody—the

Party, the people, and especially the students and intellectuals—owed a great deal to him, and so we decided to organize a memorial event and see where it would lead naturally. At least this would be something that the government couldn't stop because Yasbang had been a Party chief. We seized that moment. There was no time to think. Go. Do it.

To our surprise, the reaction was enormous. We staged a demonstration that stretched all over China. University campuses throughout the country began to link together. At first we used the telephone to network, and later we faxed. The media helped, too. The BBC, China Service, and Voice of America reported what we were doing. By listening to the radio, we knew what was going on in other cities. Large groups of student activists were gathering in Tiananmen Square, the center of Beijing. I had to be there with them.

TIANANMEN SQUARE

I arrived at the square on April 27, 1989. In the beginning it was scary. It was dangerous. It was exciting. We knew that it was entirely possible that we would be thrown into jail and disappear, like everybody else who thought differently from the Communists, including my parents and grandparents. But we students couldn't bear this life anymore. We had to try a new thing.

Our demand was a simple one. We wanted an open dialogue with the government. We were prepared to discuss three issues: freedom of the press, official corruption, and educational reform. If the government answered our call, it would have been the first time in Communist China's history

Tiananmen Square

that people had exercised the right to petition their leaders. We figured that if we could put the government on record regarding this right, it would be difficult to reverse it in the future.

At Tiananmen Square, we established a small republic. We had a university, a headquarters, and a supply center. In the center of the huge square stands a monument which became our command post. We chose leaders who represented the different universities. I was elected the head of the Student Congress on Tiananmen Square, which consisted of four hundred universities from all over China. This was the policy-making body. I was also made the deputy commander of the demonstrations.

More than two hundred thousand students and an equal number of citizens demonstrated every day. Nearby restaurants helped feed us. Residents donated food and supplies. We had a team of about two hundred people whose sole job was to bring in food. We put in place lots of portable toilets.

Throughout the day we conducted meetings and held demonstrations. We started a daily newspaper that went out to all the major residential areas. I was very excited. I slept about three, four hours a day for two months. I was so high spirited, really high spirited. It was a tremendous time, truly tremendous.

Tiananmen turned into an emotional outpouring. After forty years, we were finally able to say what was on our minds. We anticipated the beginning of a new era. We were scared and hopeful, and the atmosphere was one of heroism. As more and more people came out, we felt our strength and power. We began to say clearly what we wanted and what we did not want. We became a political movement.

One afternoon, I was standing by the monument speaking to half a million people. I was speaking very excitedly. I was passionate. At some point, I realized that I was uttering the paragraphs and sentences that I had read a long time ago in my grandfather's unpublished books. Facing the monument hung a huge portrait of Chairman Mao. I looked up and saw Mao's face staring down at me. I also saw that the people had turned their faces toward me with their backs to Mao. It was a very symbolic moment. At that moment I realized that my grandfather was speaking through my mouth. He outlived Mao. His ideas outlived Mao. My grandfather was not a madman.

People from all walks of life joined. Our movement was getting bigger and bigger and bigger. Demonstrations spread to 150 cities. More universities joined us.

We had no idea what the international community was like, but we knew that an upcoming visit by President Gorbachev of what was then the Soviet Union would be an important historical event. This was to be the first time since China and the Soviet Union had broken their relationship that the leaders of both nations would meet together. Big news.

The Communist Party leaders didn't want anything to spoil Gorbachev's visit. Students were to be arrested and expelled from universities afterward. We knew that as soon as Gorbachev left, the government was going to crack down on our group, and we would die. Everyone knew that. At the same time, there was a sense that we had come so far, and if we stopped now, nothing would be accomplished. The crackdown would come, and our ideas, our dreams would die, but if we proceeded, we might make a difference. We proposed a very risky plan that pushed the movement a step forward.

On May 13, we started a hunger strike with the hope of rallying national and international support. I was made deputy commander of the hunger strike. This began the occupation of Tiananmen Square. We set up tents for the two hundred thousand people who chose to remain in the square full time. Gorbachev arrived on the fifteenth, and with him came about three thousand journalists from around the world.

Initially, one thousand people participated in the hunger strike. In the end, it was three thousand.

We sent Gorbachev an invitation to meet with us, but he never responded. It didn't matter because the Chinese people felt so passionate and sympathetic toward us. We were willing to die for our modest demands. We risked so much for our beliefs. The hunger strike lasted until the early morning of May 20, when Deng called in the army. He imposed martial law, and two hundred thousand troops surrounded us.

We carried a heavy responsibility. Peasants, workers, and people from all stations of life considered us their leaders. Hundreds of millions of people depended on us. We were kids. I was only twenty-three at the time. The responsibility seemed too much. We all were very depressed and very scared. On the day martial law was imposed, my girlfriend joined me in Tiananmen. It was such an emotional time. I asked her, "Do you want to marry?"

"Why not?" she replied. We had our "ceremony" in the middle of the square. Our wedding was attended by 30,000 people. It was a joyful, crazy, scary time. I felt so much in love, so alive. And yet I knew that when the tanks moved in, I would die.

I was extremely worried about my wife's safety. That same day, I sent her home, accompanied by two of my best friends. Later I tried to get her out of China but failed.

On May 31 the tanks were ready to move in. There were army helicopters flying overhead. In defiance, we erected a symbolic statue called the Goddess of Democracy. There were passionate disagreements within the group about what we should do. Everybody was crazy in a sense. People were so scared.

The students overreacted, became emotional, tense, and

couldn't think clearly. I'm sure I was also crazy, but somehow I was able to maintain some sense of sanity, probably because of my experiences during the earthquake and with the lizards in the day-care center.

People didn't know how to respond to that tremendous crisis, either. Normal reactions don't apply in these kinds of situations. The Communists also were crazy. Nobody in the Party could agree on how to handle this issue. Almost everybody was sympathetic to us, even party members. Were it not for Deng Xiaoping, they would never be able to impose such a slaughter. Deng was the only one who could keep people together. He personally controlled the army. Every major post was appointed by him.

MASSACRE

June 4, 1989. Deng ordered the troops to fire. The Beijing Square massacre began. When the bloodbath started, I was standing in the center of the square. Tanks were closing in from the north. For the most part, the massacre took place on the roads leading toward Tiananmen. The tanks and troops started to move in at nine o'clock that night. They pushed forward despite the resistance of the people, killing whoever got in their way. Lots of citizens came out to protect the students, believing that they could stop the troops' movement. They were convinced that the People's Army would never fire on the people. What they didn't realize, or realized too late, was that the military was determined to kill as many people as was needed to clear the square.

The tanks and soldiers reached the square at midnight. The

citizens were able to stop and burn one tank. When I saw the tank go up in flames, I ordered all the people to remain peaceful in response to the soldiers' violence. If we were to die, we would die with dignity.

We gathered together under the monument of people's liberation in the center of the square. It was very dark. Only the burning tank gave out light. We were determined to become martyrs. After the tanks surrounded us, they stopped. It was silent for a while. We could see the glare from the soldiers' shiny helmets, but there was no movement.

At that time, a number of people suggested that we start a negotiation. Maybe there was a possible way to leave with dignity. We sent a representative to talk to the military leaders. The military promised that they wouldn't come in until seven o'clock in the morning. They allowed us to leave.

Most of the people were determined never to leave Tiananmen Square. Now, with their dream gone and so many people killed, they were ready to die with the dream. Feng Congole, Chai Ling and I were the only three leaders in the square at the time. I was convinced that to save one person was a victory. If there was a chance to leave, we all should leave together. If we chose to stay, we all must die together, right there in the center of the square. Before we could make a decision, everyone in the square had to vote. We were a democracy.

We took an oral vote. The choice was "Whoever wants to go, say 'yes.' Whoever does not want to go, say 'stay.' "

God knows which response sounded louder. My voice was gone. Chai Ling was totally exhausted. Feng Congole announced that we should go. That decision saved a lot of people. Our group of about three thousand got permission to leave by the southeast exit. It took a while to move out. But as soon as we started to go, the tanks came down from the north. I was at the top of the line. At that time we didn't know if this was a trap. The soldiers were only five meters away. About twelve people at the end of the line were crushed by the tanks. There was shooting everywhere, but not directly at people. I guess they tried to scare us.

To this day I don't know what the soldiers' orders were and I don't know *why* they let us leave the square. The tanks followed us and then went back to the center of the square. A camera crew went with them to film the demise of our Goddess of Democracy. The scene of the tank crushing the Goddess, our symbol of hope and freedom, was broadcast on TV again and again and again.

UNDERGROUND

We went directly to Beijing University, where we were told that the military was coming for us any minute. We immediately went underground. The next day the military closed every major street, especially in the university district. It was a horrendous time.

My picture began to appear everywhere on a "most wanted" list, and I went into hiding. Once I began my escape, many people recognized me. No one turned me in. That told me something. It would have been so easy for them to turn me in, but the people hid me. They were regular people whom I had never met and probably will never meet again. They helped in a big, big way. I owe them a moral debt.

I was not frightened at all. I was very depressed. There were moments when I came very close to being caught. Many people died. And I lived. I had the terrible sense that the ship had sunk and the captains were still alive. A terrible sense. Just terrible.

I traveled to southern China and, through the help of an underground network, to Hong Kong. From Hong Kong, I went to France for a few months, and then to the United States. I am presently attending my grandfather's university, Columbia University, where I am taking a joint degree in law and economics.

Many of my colleagues were sent to prison. We have no contact with them. Those who did make it out stay in touch. In New York, I spend my time at school, doing human rights work, political work, writing a book, making a documentary film, going to conferences, and working on policy papers. I want change. I want to do more. I want to be involved in the process. I want to return to China.

A Message from Lu:

After the massacre, everybody told me to let the world know about Tiananmen. Tell the world. There will be people, there will be countries that will help, because we are fighting for exactly what the modern community believes in. We let the world know and then nothing happened. I felt terribly disappointed and betrayed.

Now I don't feel that way. There is a limited amount of things one nation can do against the sovereignty of another. One thing they should not do is promise too much. If other nations stand by as sympathetic figures, expectations will be different. In the end, it is the people who must fight for what they deserve. Chinese democracy is first and foremost a Chinese thing and must be fought for by Chinese. It's a hard lesson to swallow.

CHAPTER 2

His Father's Son

BRIEFING—CUBA

In order to protect private business (mostly U.S.-owned), the United States occupied Cuba in 1906, 1912, and 1917. A period of democracy first came in 1940 under presidents Fulgencio Batista, Ramón Grau San Martín, and Carlos Prío Socarrás. This lasted for twelve years, until General Batista led a coup that established brutal, authoritarian control.

In 1959, Batista was overthrown by Dr. Fidel Castro, a young nationalist who had the popular support of the Cuban people. The United States broke off diplomatic relations the next year, after all U.S.-owned businesses were nationalized without reimbursement. A year later, the newly elected U.S. president, John F. Kennedy, ordered an invasion of Cuba (The Bay of Pigs). To the embarrassment of the administration, the invasion failed miserably. The United States tried a new tactic to bring down Castro's government by imposing a trade em-

39

bargo, which remains in effect at this writing. Castro tightened his growing relationship with the Soviet Union and proclaimed his country a Communist state. When Soviet premier Nikita Khrushchev gave Castro nuclear missiles, the Cuban Missile Crisis brought the two superpowers to the brink of nuclear war. War was averted when the Soviets backed down and agreed to dismantle the missiles.

In 1985 Mikhail Gorbachev became president of the Soviet Union. He introduced liberal reforms, attempted to reduce the arms race, and abandoned his country's support of Third World nations. As a result Cuba's economy deteriorated.

There are dozens of dissidents and human rights groups in Cuba. Hundreds of activists have been given long prison terms for spreading "enemy propaganda," a serious crime in Cuba.

David Moya

Activist—Cuba

Even today, when nobody else has a car, my father has three cars. He has two motorcycles and two houses. In my country, people are sentenced to four to seven years in prison if they are caught with fighting cocks. My father has fighting dogs and fighting cocks. It's legal for my father. Military staff would come to my house to see the fighting cocks.

It is illegal to kill a cow or a horse. You can get twenty years in prison for that. My father kills a horse, and nothing happens. In Cuba, my father is a member of a small elite. He is a member of the security department, the Cuban KGB. He works in counterintelligence and is one of the chiefs of staff.

David

My mother was a professor at the University of Havana and the assistant to the minister of education. Her godfather was the president of the Cuban Republic.

I wore blue jeans and T-shirts that my father bought for me when he went abroad. I had long hair even though my father put people in prison because they had long hair. (Long hair was considered capitalist and bourgeois.) I had lots of American and Japanese toys, but my friends had only Russian toys. Russian toys were not as good.

In 1980, my father brought home a bunch of books. The government wanted him to read the books that taught civilians how to attack political systems. He immediately locked them up in his private library and told me that I wasn't allowed to read them. I was eleven years old. When he wasn't around, I unlocked his library and started reading the books. The first book that I read was a biography of Martin Luther King, Jr. It was a very shocking book, let me tell you. First of all, it was shocking that in America there was racial discrimination. We did not have such discrimination in our country. At the same time, I thought to myself, What if I wanted to speak out about the government the way Martin Luther King spoke out? Could I do it? I began to question why the Cuban people were not allowed to read the biography of Martin Luther King.

I read Rousseau's *Social Contract.* In the beginning it was totally incomprehensible to me. I couldn't get it. I read it for the second time and got new ideas in my mind about the way governments should work. My government gave the students only *Das Kapital* by Karl Marx. It was a dense book, and I couldn't get much from it, either.

To figure out what the books meant, I got a group of friends together to study them secretly in my father's library. We passed the books around to everyone in the group. Another student's father was the chief of staff of the transport minister of Cuba. He got his father's books. Another was the son of the editor of the main newspaper in Cuba. He got books, too. We exchanged the books and shared their ideas with all the other people in our town, Vibora Park. We created a group and named it "Free Kids." The funny thing was this: We gave our group an English name, not a Spanish name. At first we called the group "Kids Free" because in Spanish the adjective goes after the noun. Our teacher laughed and said, "You stupid kids, it is 'Free Kids.'"

Later we got our teacher to translate songs by Pink Floyd. We were twelve or thirteen. Pink Floyd's "Another Brick in the Wall" became the national anthem for all the Free Kids. In time, we became a national movement, like the hippies in the United States. Our movement was more cultural than political. I especially loved the music. My favorite bands were Following Year, ACDC, and Pink Floyd.

I started writing pamphlets saying that we didn't want a dictatorship anymore. No one convinced me that my ideas were wrong. At that time, though, I couldn't tell if the evil was because of Fidel Castro or because of the whole system. I couldn't distinguish.

My father didn't know about our group at that time. When he found out about us, he and the authorities couldn't believe that we kids would ever become leaders. But then again, they also couldn't believe that the Soviet Union would collapse.

In 1982, the government put about 180 people in jail for political activities. I was one of them. I was sentenced to four years for handing out antigovernment propaganda pamphlets. They caught me in the act, and there was nothing that I could do. The pamphlets said that we wanted democracy. At that time I didn't know what democracy was, let me tell you.

I was accused of propaganda and of illegally leaving the country. I had never left the country illegally, but they accused me of that. To be honest, I was totally scared. At first, the guards didn't treat me in a very bad way, I think out of consideration for my father. They didn't torture me. That came later.

My cell was totally black, no windows, no light. I couldn't see my hand until the second day. There was a small hole in the corner for a toilet. I had to feel for it with my hands. I slept on a bunker made of cement. For two days I was alone. The authorities didn't know what to do with me. Should they treat me as a political enemy or as my father's son? They literally kept me in the dark until they made a decision. They gave me food, but I couldn't eat it because it was so nasty. It was rice, but it was full of worms. In prison I quit eating rice. One day I ate fish that made me nauseous. I opened the fish and worms came out. Until earlier this year I could not eat fish at all.

My father was informed immediately that I was in jail, but I didn't see him until ten days later. He came dressed in his military uniform. We got into an argument. When he showed up wearing military clothes, I was so disappointed in my father. I told him, "In front of me you can come naked if you want, but not like this. You come as my father or you don't come. I don't want to see you anymore." I was in jail because of his system. He was supporting the dictator.

He told me that he preferred to see me dead than against the Communists.

I said, "Well, now I'm dead because I am against the Communists." He left the place. I thought to myself, If he kicks me, I'm going to kick him back. I'm not sure I could do it, but I was very hurt.

I was sentenced to four years in prison with only a mockery of a trial. I was fifteen. At the time I was confused. I didn't understand why my father did not realize that the system was wrong. I thought that my mother lived with her eyes closed. Eventually, my mother opened her eyes because she loved me a lot. When she did, she was expelled from her job and from the Party and forced to do agricultural labor. My father did not lose power because he moved out of our house and divorced my mother. Later he remarried and divorced again.

The government offered political prisoners a "rehabilitation plan." Accepting this rehabilitation plan meant that we were wrong and they were right. During the first three or four months of my sentence, my father visited me again, without his uniform. He said, "If you accept this, you will be out in six months." I told him that I couldn't accept it because it was against my morals, against my ideals. If I thought I was wrong, I would have accepted it. But I wasn't wrong. *They* were wrong.

Prison life was very difficult. I had had asthma when I was a child, but had stopped having attacks once I turned thirteen. In prison, I had an asthma attack almost every day. Sometimes they gave me my medicine and sometimes they didn't. When I asked for medicine for another prisoner because he was dying, they beat me. I lost a tooth. Another time, I was kicked in my testicles. They got so big that they wouldn't fit into my pants. I had never been treated as an animal before. I had been treated as a millionaire. Now I was only a number.

We were twelve people living in a twelve-meter-square cell.

Several important persons were in this group, including teachers from the University of Havana and two ambassadors. My prisoner friends and I began to exchange things. "You don't mind the rice? I'll give you the rice and you give me the bread."

We all shared one vice—cigarettes. We tried to quit smoking. When visitors brought me cigarettes, I exchanged them for books. We exchanged things with the common [nonpolitical] prisoners. Cigarettes for books. Cigarettes for pencils. Cigarettes for paper.

We had a person who had been a sports leader in Cuban society. He set up an exercise program for each person according to their body weight. We started doing exercises so as not to lose strength.

I had an incredible education in jail. We got books in English, French, Italian. I learned French and English with a dictionary. Not even Gustavo, who had been the ambassador to Belgium and was later nominated for a Nobel Peace Prize, knew how to speak English. Emilio, who was once ambassador to a Soviet republic, knew a little and became the teacher. We guessed at the pronunciation of the words. For example, the word *even:* I say, "e-*vant.*"

We read philosophy books. We began what later became our Human Rights University, where we taught people what their rights were. We put together a magazine that we called *Exodus.* We'd write out about seven copies by hand and pass it around to the other inmates.

Then we created the Cuban Human Rights Committee, an ongoing illegal organization that is now trying to get recognized by Geneva's International Commission for Human Rights. I was the youngest member. The Human Rights Committee was the beginning of everything. We exchanged letters with Václav Havel. We exchanged letters with Andrei Sakharov's widow, Elena Bonner. [Andrei Sakharov, a Soviet physicist, won the Nobel Peace Prize in 1975.]

It was illegal to have a copy of the United Nations' Human Rights Declaration. We managed to get a copy of it from government officials who published it for their Cuban lawyers working in embassies abroad. With the declaration as our guide, we created a small government, complete with a constitution and officers. There were five representatives, one president, and one vice president. I was made the secretary because I was the youngest.

One time my girlfriend was smuggled into prison to see me. Her father found out about it. He dragged her by the hair and smashed her face into the refrigerator. He broke her nose. He broke her teeth. She was totally deformed after he hit her. I don't know if her father did that because he was afraid not to, or because he loved Fidel. I think because he loved Fidel Castro. My girlfriend wrote me a letter saying she never wanted to see me again, and took it to my mother's house. When my mother saw her, she started crying.

My mother brought me the letter. I felt so bad because the beating was my fault. My girlfriend had all this trouble because of me. It was a very bad time.

From fifteen to nineteen, I couldn't have sex because I was in jail. I couldn't have girlfriends because I was in jail. That was hard, let me tell you. Actually, I didn't want anybody to be my girlfriend. Just because I chose to suffer for an ideal didn't mean that another person should suffer for it, too.

After I spent eight months in prison, the authorities tried to separate our group. We went on a hunger strike for twelve days, seven without water. We didn't want to be split up and put in with common prisoners who might try to abuse the young people. We wanted to keep together as a family. Surprisingly, we won the hunger strike.

International newspapers were important to us. They had agencies in Havana. The ambassadors in our group knew how things worked and taught us to record events just like on police reports. "Eleven o'clock, this happened . . . One minute after eleven, this happened . . ." It was so primitive. We were like children learning to walk. We'd lean to one side and then the other until, little by little, we began walking straight.

The funny thing was this: We were living a Communist life even though we were against the Communists. Inside the prison, if someone got candy, they shared that candy with you. Everybody smoked from the same cigarette. (We didn't entirely conquer our vice.)

After four years, I was released from prison. By that time our Human Rights Committee had more than two hundred members. *Radio Martí,* which is part of Voice of America, started transmitting news from the United States.

For nine months I was out of prison and living in my mother's house. She was still doing agricultural work but coming back to the house where I grew up. I started doing human rights work again. I bought an old typewriter and began writing. Our group gave out information about prison life to the media. I began collecting books for the prisoners who were left behind. We made some contact with several guards and bribed them to bring the books into the prison.

The authorities didn't allow me to return to school, or to

work. My mother supported me. It was very difficult. I was forced to sell my possessions, which is illegal in Cuba. I sold the blue jeans that my father bought me when I was young. Some of them still fit me, but I sold them to have money to live.

Other times we brought food to the prisoners. Powdered milk, sugar, medicine. Families called to ask what to take during a visit to an inmate. We also arranged transportation for families without cars. We helped the families and we helped the prisoners. At the same time, we helped society by giving it a conscience.

Several lawyers in our committee taught us the difference between international law and Cuban law. We taught people what to do if they were sent to prison, what to tell the interviewer, what their rights were. Everything was written and certified and put into our human rights constitution.

Another thing we did was change the name of Free Kids. The government had put secret agents inside Free Kids who tried to discredit us by calling themselves "Free Kiss." They tried to make the group look bad. They succeeded. At this moment, it is a bad group in Cuba.

By 1986, the foreign press loved writing about me because I had been the youngest prisoner and because my father was in the government. I had to keep speaking out. It was the moral thing to do. Then, in 1987, they arrested me again.

I was charged with counterrevolutionary activities and sentenced to two years in prison. I was around twenty. This time it was very easy for me. I was used to prison, so I was prepared. When the car braked in front of my house at seven in the morning, I knew I was leaving for jail. When they were about to knock, I opened the door and said, "Take me."

This time, the authorities decided to have a public trial. There were three judges, two young people and an older one. The prosecuting lawyer was an official of the government. I was assigned a lawyer who never once visited me in prison. He knew nothing about my case. I said, "This person cannot defend me because he is a military official. He's worried about being arrested himself. How the hell is he going to defend a person who opposes his revolution?" The judges got together and decided that I could defend myself. I think this is the first time the government allowed somebody to defend himself. And the funny thing is this: I think it is the last time they did that, too.

This was my chance to tell the government about their violations against me and the people. One hundred people were in the court. My mother was there and my father was there. When it was my turn to speak, I took from my pocket the United Nations Declaration of Human Rights. I explained that the government of Cuba signed this declaration, and I wanted to compare this to the Cuban constitution. I talked about each article and showed how the Cuban constitution worked contrary to it. When I reached Article 21, they told me to shut up.

"That's part of the government's rules: to shut people up and to keep people silent," I responded. The moment I finished, everybody started clapping. The government was really pissed off.

I think my sentence ended up being only one year and six months because I made so much trouble in prison that the government decided to let me out.

I started a movement inside prison. People who were leaving the country illegally were considered common prisoners. I tried to get all these people together. We held another hunger strike. More than a hundred people participated, even the ordinary prisoners. It was a pacifist way. No fighting. No violence. We tried to follow the teachings of Martin Luther King, Jr., Mahatma Gandhi, and Christ.

One thing we tried to do inside the prison was to show the guards that we were fighting for their rights, too. In the beginning the guards were very, very suspicious. They didn't want to talk to us. Then, little by little, they started doing things for us. For example, it is illegal to have a radio inside the prison. We got money illegally from our families and gave it to the guards to buy us a radio.

Some of the guards were better than others. The same guard who brought me the radio would kill me if he was told to do it. That's the system. When I was alone with one guard, we were friends. He'd talk to me like a brother. Later, he was ordered to kick me and beat me. He beat me hard. They did it in groups, and if he didn't beat me hard, they would get him in trouble.

After one guard beat me, I said, "Don't be ashamed. I know your position." Then, the second time he had to beat me, he was very demoralized.

Once a guard started crying. He said, "I cannot stand this anymore." He was kicking another person and I interfered. Other guards came and kicked me, too. Later, I called to him and said, "I know that if you don't do it, they are going to put you in jail."

My third imprisonment, in 1989, was my worst time. Once again I was sentenced for counterrevolutionary activities. We started a magazine called *Franqueca,* which means *"glas-*

nost." I was one of the editors of the magazine. It was more like a newspaper, with two pages printed every week. I had many contacts with ambassadors and foreign secretaries at different embassies in Cuba. Because I spoke a little English, I became the person who met with the media. We also met with four American senators who went to Cuba to talk to Fidel Castro and the opposition.

Our group held the first democratic election in Cuba. We sent out a paper asking people to sign up to vote for a multi-party system. This would have been the first plebiscite in Cuba. We sent that paper to all the members of our human rights group. Ten thousand people signed up to vote. Let me tell you, that was very, very rare in Cuba.

On the day of the vote, I was supervising the voting process at one of three voting stations. My post was at the house of Edita Esther. (Edita was a member of the party. Her husband had been a doctor who was thrown out of his job when the government discovered that he was a member of the human rights movement. They now live in Venezuela.) I walked onto Edita's balcony, looked down at all the people lining up to vote, and thought to myself that democracy was coming to Cuba. I was twenty-two years old and taking this group toward democracy. Let me tell you, it was everything for me.

The secret police were outside the house. They were not friendly, but they were not willing to take us off to prison. A month later they arrested me again.

On April 4, President Gorbachev of the Soviet Union was visiting Cuba. Foreign journalists were allowed into Cuba to cover the event. They arrived March 29. For five days our group held several conferences with CNN, *Radio Martí,* ABC, and the print media.

At one point we called for a major human rights demonstration in front of the Soviet embassy. We knew this would be denied by the government, but we did it anyway. I formally petitioned the Number 5 Police Station in Miramar, a district in Havana where the government people live and most of the embassies are located, to hold a legal demonstration.

Pablo Gato, a journalist from a Spanish-language television station in the United States, and other reporters came with me. When the police saw me arrive with the cameras and the press, they thought that I was a member of the government. They saluted me in military style. It was really funny. Once they realized that I was a member of the opposition, everything changed. They threw the press out and kept me inside the police station. While I was there, I gave them the formal petition. It was denied and I was sent home.

On April 4, a huge ring of police encircled the blocks leading to the Soviet embassy. Anybody even walking near the area was immediately arrested. Around three o'clock in the morning, the police arrested about twenty leaders of the Human Rights Party, including me.

Cuban law says that when a person is arrested, he must be taken to the security department or the police station nearest to his town. The police took us from our town and moved us far away, to an eastern municipality. My mother and our families asked where we were. The press asked, too. The government refused to say where we were. My father knew where I was because he was part of the government, but he would not tell my mother. I was sentenced to prison for leading an illegal organization.

At first I was sentenced to three years. Then they added an additional six years because every time I did something in prison, they increased my term. One day I wrote a letter to the warden. "What is the longest sentence in Cuba that exists? I'm going to surpass that sentence."

The government considered me a political enemy and really wanted to destroy me. They put me with the most hardened criminals in the expectation that they would sexually harass and even kill me. The meanest, worst prisoner was put in a cell with me. But something interesting happened. One of the prisoners knew me from my town. He became like a bodyguard for me, and no one was able to sexually harass me. The police thought they had a perfect informer in my "bodyguard," but what they really had was someone who protected me.

I decided to get smart and play professional baseball [play hardball]. I started giving my cell mate information, which he turned over to the police. At the same time, I smuggled this same information to the press. For example, if a guard beat a particular person, I'd write two copies of a denunciation. Copy one, I gave to my "bodyguard," who turned it over to the police. Copy two, I gave to someone who smuggled it out to the press. I always gave out true information because if it was fake, they would suspect something.

At one point I asked to have a priest visit me in my cell. When the authorities refused my request, I held a hunger strike. This was the first time in that jail that a prisoner was allowed to receive a priest. The priest came back to see me a second time, but I wasn't allowed to see him. A day earlier I had been beaten by the guards so badly that my face, my eyes, and my back were purple. That's a very sad chapter in my life. I wanted to receive the priest and I wasn't allowed to see him because I was totally beaten up.

One day the police made a big mistake. They gave the

54

informer a letter telling him to hurt me, and he gave me the letter. It was very brave of him. He had been sentenced to forty-eight years for killing three people. I smuggled the letter outside and then asked for a meeting of the whole staff of the security department of the KGB.

They came. I said, "I have this letter where Enrique Gonzales, the warden of the prison, wrote to this prisoner telling him to hurt me. I sent it out of the prison, and if you hurt me, it is going to be published."

The next thing that happened is that my bodyguard was released, although he had served only twelve years of his sentence. In Cuba there is no parole, so he still had thirty-six years to go. He was let free because he knew too much and because they didn't want him to be close to me.

I was totally isolated. I went for days without seeing anybody. Then, all of a sudden, I was treated like a human being again. I thought, Something's going on. I didn't know that I had been given an international human rights award. That's what actually got me out of prison.

Coordinadora de Derechos Humanos had proposed that I receive the Reebok Human Rights Award. The Reebok Human Rights Foundation gave me their award and wrote a letter to the Cuban government asking for my release. Both Reebok and Amnesty International sent letters on my behalf. Castro received more than five thousand letters from their international members. Organizations in Miami worked very hard for my release, too, including the *Comite Cubano Pro Derechos Humanos*. Americas Watch, who had mentioned me every year in their list of prisoners of conscience, mounted a big campaign for me.

What probably saved my life was the fact that I was known

in the international human rights community, had contacts in the press, and a father in the government. I was one of the lucky ones.

The deal was that I had to leave the country. By that time I had been sentenced to twenty-nine years and six months. The government bowed to international pressure. Publicly, they say they don't care about international pressure, but they do. It worked with me and it has worked with other people.

I was given ninety days to remain in the country, otherwise I would have to go back to prison. The United States Interest Office gave me a humanitarian visa. [There is no U.S. embassy in Cuba.] It was the first time I had a visa. I didn't want to leave my country, and I said that I was not going, I was going to stay in Cuba. On the eighty-seventh day, I was informed that if I remained in the country I was going back to jail. Then my father did something nice. He came and told me, "They are going to kill you, and I can do nothing. They are going to kill you because you are doing too much. Either you leave and live, or stay and be killed."

When my father told me that, it was like a reconciliation, because he was acting like a father again. I forgave him, he forgave me. Maybe I was too hard on him. Maybe he was too hard on me. All my friends, the leaders of the Human Rights Party, left Cuba. And I left, too.

I flew to America. The director of the Reebok Human Rights Foundation was waiting for me at the airport. There were lots of newspeople. I had met many of them before. (The day I left Cuba, my bodyguard was picked up by the police and taken back to jail. His mother lives in Miami, and I visit her all the time.)

I don't talk about the past with my father. We love each other. I think he loves me. I don't hate him. I don't even hate Fidel Castro. I hate the system that makes people suffer so much. It's not the person, it's the system. It doesn't matter if it is left or right, it's the same.

I'd love to go back to Cuba. I want to go as soon as I can. I want to go back because the battle is there.

A MESSAGE FROM DAVID:

Write letters to dictators. Write letters to violators of human rights. It works.

II
Freedom from Communal Violence

In the present Convention, genocide [a crime under international law] means any of the following acts committed with intent to destroy, in whole or in part, a national, ethical, racial or religious group, as such:

(a) Killing members of the group;

(b) Causing serious bodily or mental harm to members of the group;

(c) Deliberately inflicting on the group conditions of life calculated to bring about its physical destruction in whole or in part;

(d) Imposing measures intended to prevent births within the group;

(e) Forcibly transferring children of the group to another group.

Convention on the Prevention and Punishment of the Crime of Genocide, Article 2

Chapter 3

Working in a War Zone

BRIEFING—BOSNIA

Researchers from Human Rights Watch travel to more than seventy countries to interview victims of human rights abuses. These interviews make up the heart of reports that are sent to heads of state, ambassadors, politicians, journalists, and other interested parties. Take the case of the former Yugoslavia.

Yugoslavia was made up of six separate republics: Bosnia-Hercegovina, Serbia, Croatia, Slovenia, Montenegro, and Macedonia. Bosnia-Hercegovina declared its independence on April 6, 1992. As soon as the international community recognized the new state, armed conflict followed.[1]

As a result of this conflict, people all over the world became familiar with the phrase "ethnic cleansing." Ethnic cleansing is the removal of an ethnic group by the use of force, murder, and other extreme methods of harassment.

To document this, researcher Ivana Nizich and her col-

leagues returned again and again to Bosnia, Croatia, and Serbia, even when the war was raging. They collected evidence from witnesses, visited sites where abuses took place, analyzed the gathered material, and reported their findings for Human Rights Watch. They developed material for a two-volume study about war crimes in Bosnia-Hercegovina.

Ivana Nizich
Research Associate for Human Rights Watch/Helsinki

You don't just wake up one day and decide to slit another group's throats. Obviously, there always have been differences between the various ethnic communities in Yugoslavia. They all didn't live happily together. But in the past they were not at one another's throats, just waiting to slaughter each other. They were goaded into it by leaders who were trying to take power, stay in power, or gain territory.

There are numerous opinions about how this war began. Some say that the conflict goes back to the Second World War, when the Croatian and Muslim Fascists aligned with the Nazis to slaughter Serbs, while others claim that the Serbian minority were rebelling because they were abused in both Bosnia and Croatia. Some claim it started when the Slovenes and the Croats declared their independence, while others say that it came with the political rise of the Nationalist-Communist president of the Republic of Serbia, Slobodan Milosevic. In my opinion, this is a war about territory and the maintenance of political power. Milosevic decided to take over territory and

exploited negative aspects of nationalism as a way to support his political aims.

For nearly five years I've been monitoring the former Yugoslavia. I've traveled through Serbian- , Croatian- , and Muslim-controlled areas to record victims' testimonies of human rights abuses. The Serbs don't like me much. They say that I'm anti-Serbian because my heritage is Croatian. They also think that I am pro-Muslim. Croats don't care for me, either. When my reports criticize their government or their armed forces, they say that I am biased. They tell me that I'm a self-hater. "Okay, guys," I say, "first of all, I wasn't born or raised there. My parents left Yugoslavia in the fifties. I'm a New Yorker." This argument doesn't penetrate one bit.

The Muslims don't seem to have much of a problem with me. I criticize them, too, but they accept it relatively okay. They've even taken steps to correct some of their abuses. They need to take many more steps, but they're not as hostile as Serbian forces.

Prior to these events, of the 4.35 million people who lived in the area [Bosnia-Hercegovina], 43.7 percent were Slavic Muslims, 31.3 percent Serbs, and 17.3 percent Croats. The rest were other minorities.[2]

The Serbs haven't given us access to their occupied zones for quite a while. Earlier my colleagues and I were able to get in. Then we'd get kicked out, and we'd go in again. Nobody would talk to us. We'd be threatened, but everybody gets threatened.

I go into war-torn areas. I'm not the only one: there are three other people who work with me. Our little group is made up

63

of two local monitors (one Serb and one Croat) and two foreigners. There have been times when I've worked alone, but I don't drive a stick shift very well, so I have to find somebody to drive with me.

We go to places where abuses have taken place, where people have been displaced. We just get in a car and drive around, like tourists. Usually people look at us and think we're insane because we don't have an armored vehicle. We drive in a soft-skin vehicle [a car]. We do not go into places like Sarajevo in a soft-skin vehicle. No way. When we go there, we take a U.N. flight—or did when they existed. It may sound glamorous, but it's not. There is nothing glamorous about what's happening in Bosnia.

We don't go into the thick of a battle. That's for journalists and photojournalists. At times like that, who can we help? We can't get testimony because people can't take time out from a war to document experiences. We go into an area and begin interviewing as soon after an incident as possible. It helps a lot that we all speak the language, even though I have a heavy accent, so we don't need to rely on translators.

My colleagues and I will not interview anybody if we think our presence will endanger them. A few journalists—some, not many—have interviewed Muslims in Serb-held territory. They leave and the next day the Muslims are beaten, shot, killed, or interrogated because they were talking to foreigners. We're less prominent than foreign journalists because we don't come in with a whole camera crew or with an armored vehicle.

A long time is spent talking to each person. Everything must be carefully described and detailed. We try to do spontaneous interviews, preferably with people who have not been interviewed before. The more people are interviewed, the more fine-tuned, or exaggerated, their stories become.

The ideal situation is first to talk to a few people to get an idea of what went on. Second, go to the actual site and take a look at the terrain, because it's good to have a mental picture of the geography of the area. Then go back and interview more people.

In a way, my job is rather technical. I try to determine what's a deliberate abuse, what's an indiscriminate abuse, and what's a disproportionate response. For example, when an allegation is made that a town was totally destroyed by an aerial attack, we visit the site to see what damage resulted from the bombing. If there's not a lot of damage (structures are still standing, no craters in the roads), I report that the allegation has been exaggerated. We spend about 70 percent of our time investigating true human rights abuses; about 30 percent of the allegations are exaggerated.

Even though the situation is terrible, it is not considered a human rights violation in a strictly legal sense when people leave their homes because of the fighting. But if somebody goes to a person's house and says, "You're the wrong ethnic group . . . you are the wrong religion . . . you *have* to leave," that's a human rights abuse.

Early Warnings

In early 1991, I was in Belgrade [the capital of Serbia]. There were outbreaks of fighting in parts of Croatia between Croatian police and Serbian paramilitaries. One night I was watching the government-controlled TV news. The program gave the impression that Croat police officers massacred all the Serbs in a Croatian town. I telephoned some Croatian people I know in Zagreb [the capital of Croatia] and screamed, "What are you people doing? Why are you abusing the Serbs?"

They said, "Wait a minute. Wait a minute. They attacked the police station first. They came in with AK-47s. The battle was between the police and armed Serbians. We didn't go out and slaughter Serbs."

My human rights colleagues and I went to the site of the fighting to see for ourselves what happened. We interviewed Serbs and Croats. On the basis of the testimony from both sides, we learned that, contrary to the televised report, the Serbian troops attacked the Croatian police. This was a scuffle between the local police and armed Serbian rebels. There was no massacre of Serbian civilians. Even the Serbs living there told me this. Most of what I saw on Belgrade TV had been a lie.

I used to believe most of what the media said. Now I don't believe anything. When I see something on TV, I am inclined to think the opposite is true. If I believed these stories, imagine what the person in a remote village in Serbia watching the evening TV news believes. Government-sponsored programs are their main source of information.

GETTING INFORMATION

Generally people will talk to me. Whether they are professionals (professors, lawyers, doctors, engineers) or farmers and peasants who work the land, their experiences tend to be similar. They are in their village or town when shelling starts. The shelling continues for several days, several weeks, several

Ivana at work

months. Some people flee, while others stay in their homes. Soldiers arrive and execute a few people as a way of intimidating the others. They take the remaining men to camps. Women and children are separated. Some are let go, others are sent to other camps.

Because there is a war going on, we monitors sometimes need a permit to get around. The first thing we do is go to the army headquarters and ask for a "freedom of movement" pass. Then, when we are stopped at a roadblock, we have something to show the soldiers. We are sometimes told, "We can't guarantee your safety and can't give you a pass," i.e., if somebody wants to shoot you, more power to them. That's the attitude.

People who were abused by Serbian troops, and survived, are usually willing to talk to us. We interviewed literally hundreds and hundreds of people. Then we returned home and wrote two books and other reports about the area that are litanies of horrors.

The Camps

All parties to the conflict have mistreated persons held in detention facilities under their control. Prisoners have been summarily executed, beaten (sometimes to death), raped, starved, sexually humiliated, and otherwise mistreated in detention in Bosnia-Hercegovina.

Military and police forces of the self-proclaimed "Serbian Republic" of Bosnia-Hercegovina detained prisoners in four detention camps in northwestern Bosnia, which were subsequently closed as a result of international condemnation. In two of the camps—Omarska and Keraterm—detained persons, primarily men, were regularly beaten to death, starved, and terrorized.[3]

In order to get into detention camps, we need permission from the authorities who control the camps. We go to the local military post and tell the commander who we are and what we want to do. Usually they let us in. Sometimes they tell us to drop dead or get lost (usually the Serbian authorities tell us that).

Selima [a Bosnian Muslim] was picked up again and sent to Keraterm camp and then transferred to Omarska. Before she was taken to Omarska, she had spent two nights locked in a van in Keraterm, where she previously had been raped. Selima and one other woman were taken to Omarska with other male prisoners from Keraterm. During the ride to Omarska,

Selima claims that a Serbian soldier [named Dragan Mrdja] beat the male prisoners. Selima spent fifty days at Omarska. . . .

"It was the most horrible place you can imagine. I watched my children being beaten, and I couldn't cry. They were killing and torturing all the time. We women stayed in this restaurant, which had a glass wall. We were ordered to sit and watch how they beat and tortured our men all morning. We slept in offices above this restaurant and, during the day, they [the officers] were used for so-called interrogations, that is, for torture. Through this [glass] wall, I could see them moving dead bodies from one part of the camp to another [section]."[4]

RAPE

Many in the human rights community believe that there won't be peace unless the abuses brought about by ethnic cleansing are resolved and rectified. Mass rape is one of them.

Each of the parties to the conflict in Bosnia-Hercegovina has used rape as a weapon of war. Soldiers attacking villages have raped women and girls in their homes, in front of family members, and in the village square. Women have been arrested and raped during interrogation. In some villages and towns, women and girls have been gathered together and taken to holding centers—often schools or com-

munity sports halls—where they are raped, gang-raped, and abused repeatedly, sometimes for days or even weeks at a time. Other women have been taken seemingly at random from their communities or out of a group of refugees with which they are traveling, and raped by soldiers.

Whether a woman is raped by soldiers in her home or is held in a house with other women and raped over and over again, she is raped with a political purpose—to intimidate, humiliate, and degrade her and others affected by her suffering. The effect of rape is often to ensure that women and their families will flee and never return.[5]

Rape in Bosnia is targeted at the opposing ethnic group. In general, Muslim soldiers don't rape Muslim women, Croat soldiers don't rape Croat women, and Serbian soldiers don't rape Serbian women. There are individual cases of drunken soldiers doing this, but that I would consider an individual criminal act.

There is sexual abuse of men as well, though it is not as widespread as the rape of women. But that goes on in the camps. It's more about humiliation. The soldiers force men to perform fellatio on one another. There are stories about castration. Male soldiers don't rape male prisoners. That I haven't heard of, yet.

According to B., a forty-year-old Muslim woman from Doboj, the Serbian soldiers had a list from which they called out women's names; they directed these women to board buses. Some children ap-

peared to have boarded the buses with their mothers. The men were left standing in a group. . . .

B. *was transferred to a high school in the Usara section of Doboj, where she was held for twenty-eight days . . .* "It began there as soon as I arrived. They told us not to look at the soldiers so that we wouldn't remember them. We were not allowed to talk with each other. During the day, we stayed in a big sports hall. The guards were always there. If they caught us talking, they would take a woman out, beat her, and more than the usual [number of men] would rape her. They liked to punish us. They would ask women if they had male relatives in the city. I saw them ask this of one woman, and they brought her fourteen-year-old son and forced him to rape her. . . .

"Some of the local Serbs wore black stockings on their heads to disguise their faces because they didn't want to be recognized. [Nevertheless] I recognized many of them. [They were] colleagues—doctors with whom I worked. The first [man] who raped me was a Serbian doctor named Jodic. He knew I recognized him. He saw my name on the list and called it out. I had known Jodic for ten years. We worked in the same hospital. I would see him every day in the employees' cafeteria. We spoke generally, 'Hi, how are you?' He was a very polite, nice man. Another doctor whom I had previously known also raped me; [his name was] Obrad Filipovic. I wasn't allowed to say anything. Before he raped me he said, 'Now you

know who we are. You will remember forever.' I was
so surprised; he was a doctor!"

B. claims that women were most frequently raped
in the classrooms of the high school. "Once I saw the
face of a woman I knew; her daughter was with her.
Three men were with them inside [the classroom]. I
was brought in by one man, and another four men
followed. On that occasion, I was raped with a gun
by one of the three men already in the room. I didn't
recognize him. Others stood watching. Some spat on
us. They were raping me, the mother, and her daugh-
ter at the same time. Sometimes you had to accept ten
men, sometimes three. Sometimes when they were
away, they wouldn't call me for one or two days. I
wanted nothing, not bread, not water, just to be
alone. I felt I wanted to die. We had no change of
clothes and couldn't wash ourselves."[6]

I've never seen so much attention devoted to one abuse
with so little action. Tens of thousands of U.N. troops are in the
area. Everybody and their grandmother are in there. Everybody and their grandmother wrote a book, or an article, or put
on a play about what is happening. Has it helped these people? It hasn't helped them with anything. Zero. Zip.

I do, however, think that this war is important for making
people finally admit that the raping of women may not be used
as a kind of booty available to the soldiers of a conquering
army. It is a war crime.

The victims that I dealt with were traumatized by the rape,
but that was not all that they had suffered. Their husbands

were killed. Their sons were incarcerated in detention camps. Their daughters were raped while they were forced to watch. They were refugees where they had little help, little food, little clothing.

With one exception, the women I interviewed told me that their families had not shunned them after they were raped. Quite the contrary. They said that their families were very supportive.

> *My husband nursed me; he was very good to me. Even now, he takes very good care of me. The following morning, he informed the police about what happened. They sent a car, which took me to the hospital. The doctor was a Serb; at that time, all Muslim physicians had been fired. He gave me shots and some powders.*
>
> "K. S."[7]

What did get blown out of proportion was the idea that these women were raped so that they would have Serbian babies. Where are these kids? I haven't seen many such children anywhere. Besides, what's the point? A Serbian man rapes a Muslim and then lets her go. She returns to Muslim-held territory where she has the child. Is that kid going to be raised as a Serb? No. It's going to be raised as a Muslim. So, the logic behind that is ridiculous. A number of women whom we interviewed told us that as they were raped, the men said, "Now you are going to bear Serbian children." To me, that sounded more like a method of intimidation than a calculated policy. A lot of people disagree with me on this.

Some of the women who did become impregnated put their

children up for adoption. A few kept them. The vast majority—Catholics, Muslims, and Orthodox—had abortions. Some women were raped and kept in detention until their third trimester. When they got out, they insisted that doctors perform abortions, even though it was illegal and dangerous at that late date. One doctor told me, "Yes, it is illegal, but I don't blame these women." The abortions were performed safely.

WRITING REPORTS

In the field, my adrenaline is working overtime and I live like everybody else lives. I record horror stories, but even so, it is easier for me to work in the field than return home and write my report. Every time I return to New York, I experience a bit of culture shock.

While I'm writing I become completely detached, as if another person were writing about the people I met. I become critical. I question everything that the interviewee told me.

If you talk to any researchers at Human Rights Watch, we are all passionate about the countries on which we work. But the minute we let that interfere with our reporting, we shouldn't be in this business. An objective standard based on international law has to apply. We can't bend and mold facts to suit political or emotional preferences.

After I've finished my last draft and I give it a final read-through, I am no longer immersed in the technicalities of the abuse. That's when it gets to me. I see faces. I wonder what happened to so-and-so. I remember the individual behind the horrible testimony.

There are some things that we do that are really worthwhile. In one Croatian-operated camp, we interviewed a number of

Muslim detainees. About seven or eight months later, when the war between the Muslims and Croats had stopped, I was back in my office in New York. The phone rang. The caller was in Sarajevo. How he got through to New York, I have no idea. He said, "Hi I'm so-and-so. You interviewed me in the Rodoc camp a few months ago. One day the guards gave us newspapers and I read your report that appeared in the Croatian press. I just wanted to thank you. You told me you wouldn't use my name and you didn't, but I knew it was me because I remember what I told you. If you ever come to Sarajevo, please look me up."

My colleague interviewed one young Croatian boy in a refugee camp who had gotten the living shit kicked out of him at Banja Luka in northwestern Bosnia. He evidently got refugee status from the U.S. and was now living in Texas. He sent my colleague a postcard from Dallas saying, "Hi, how are you doing? If you ever come down, come and visit me. Thanks for interviewing me."

Sometimes when I go across a front line, a mother will ask me to take a letter to her daughter. I'll do that so long as I know that she is not putting anything in the letter that would compromise the mission. I won't take large, wrapped packages. Usually people ask us to take chocolates across. Nobody wraps the packages because they know that they will be checked.

I also will go across the line and call up somebody to say, "I saw your mother on the other side. She wants to know how you are." We do this a lot. This is the only thing we can do except write our reports. That's the only direct personal gratification we get.

We do not deserve credit. The local people who do human

rights work under repressive regimes deserve credit. They are the ones being targeted and shot. I really admire the Serbian human rights workers. They do wonderful, wonderful work, and yet they are demonized as traitors to the nation because they dare to speak out and criticize their country's policies. They are harassed; they are beaten. They live through one horrible situation after another. I take my hat off to them.

I'm a foreigner with a foreign passport. I can come and go. I can't compare my experiences to theirs at all. It's not the same for me as it is for any of the local monitors. What happens to us is merely an inconvenience. For them, it's their life.

SARAJEVO

During the 1993 "cease-fire," I spent a month in Sarajevo. It freaked me out that we could be just sitting in our rooms and a sniper could blow our brains out. People would go out to buy a piece of bread, not knowing if they would return. As I walked down the street, guns were staring at me. That kind of psychological terror is horrifying. Can you imagine what it's like for the people who cannot leave? The people of Sarajevo have no windows, no heat, and very little food. People burn their books for heat. The U.N., to its credit, put up a lot of plastic sheeting, but still, there was no heat.

One day, a colleague and I were walking down the street and we met a professor. He was selling his books. He didn't want to part with one particular book, but he needed the money. We gave him the money and told him to keep the book. He said, "No, no, no, I can't take your money unless you take the book. Take the book." We said, "It's okay, it's okay, keep it." We were arguing back and forth. He insisted that we take it. It was heartbreaking.

We visit people's homes in Sarajevo. It's a custom to feed guests Turkish coffee and some kind of baked goods. If we don't eat, they become insulted. These people have nothing to eat themselves. We tell them that we will eat when we go home. They insist. Everybody insists, whether they are Serbs, Muslims, or Croats. These are good-hearted people living in the wrong place at the wrong time with psychotic leaders.

ABOUT IVANA

I became interested in human rights because of my kid brother. He is mentally retarded and physically handicapped. We have always been very close. Because of him I became interested in the handicapped rights movement. That led to an interest in civil liberties. I went to graduate school at Columbia University, where there was a program that combined domestic and international human rights. I'm not a lawyer. I should go to law school but I haven't gotten around to it yet. Actually, I was interested in the Middle East, but I don't speak Hebrew or Arabic. I speak Serbo-Croatian, some Russian, and some French, so I ended up in Eastern Europe. And then this war broke out.

A MESSAGE FROM IVANA

Don't buy into stereotypes. Don't assume that someone is evil because they are members of a certain religion, race, or ethnic group. If you have not been exposed to a group, don't pre-judge it. Questioning is healthy. Don't take for granted what everybody tells you, even your leaders. Especially your leaders.

CHAPTER 4

Take Care of My Children

BRIEFING—RWANDA

On the morning of April 20, 1994, the conference room at the New York offices of Human Rights Watch is packed with trustees, monitors, staff, friends, and visitors from other human rights organizations. Suddenly the door opens. Everyone jumps to their feet, applauding, cheering, and straining their necks to get their first glimpse of the stately African woman who enters.

She looks like a queen. Her smile is dazzling, despite the fact that her face is scarred from an assassination attempt. She wears a mustard yellow ceremonial gown with orange, green, and white abstract flower patterns. Her hair is carefully corn-rowed in a traditional African style.

Last year Monique Mujawamariya, a human rights monitor from Kigalie, Rwanda, was honored as one of the recipients of the Human Rights Watch Monitors' Award for "courageous

work in defending human rights in their own countries despite what are often very grave risks."

After she received her award, Monique visited the United Nations, the White House, and the State Department, where she warned the powers that be about terrible events that she was sure were going to take place in her country. Everyone listened to her message of doom. Presidents and diplomats were charmed by her spirited personality. But when the chips were down, nobody responded.

At this point in time, her warnings of mass killings have proved tragically accurate. She begins her presentation to her friends in the conference room, many of whom helped her through her terrifying ordeal. She says, "Merci, merci, merci. . . ."

Monique Mujawamariya
NGO—Rwanda

All day, every day, messages of hate were delivered on the national radio in Rwanda. "Take up your machetes. You know who the enemy is. Now is the time. The graves are only half-full." An intensive propaganda campaign was conducted in the newspapers and other media.

For two years I had been demanding that the government of Rwanda stop requiring its people to carry identity cards that indicate their ethnic origin: Hutu or Tutsi. Recently I saw a man with a machete checking people's cards as they walked by. Everyone who had a T [for Tutsi] on the card was killed. If

81

those cards had been suppressed two years ago when we reported it, or if the United States had insisted that the practice be stopped, there would have been no way of knowing which group was passing on the road. Many lives would have been spared.

I created a human rights organization in November 1990, when war began in Rwanda. Whenever there was trouble, I would investigate what had happened. I wrote reports that included the testimonies of victims and perpetrators. I proposed possible solutions to the situation. I spoke out and put pressure on the government by writing letters or directly confronting the authorities. I also made my reports available to our partners concerned with human rights in other countries, including Human Rights Watch and Amnesty International.

The conflict that is reported between the two Rwandan ethnic groups—Hutu and Tutsi—is a false problem. In our daily lives we understand each other and cohabit peacefully. You can't distinguish who belongs to what group. I am a product of a marriage between a Hutu and Tutsi. There are many such marriages in my country. We share the same language, the same culture, and even the same racial roots.

> *Prior to the twentieth century, the definition of a Hutu or a Tutsi referred to a person's economic status. A person with more than ten cows was Tutsi. A person with fewer than ten cows was Hutu.*

When the authorities wanted to hold on to their power, they sparked conflict. To spark a conflict, you chose one of the ethnic groups to favor. You gave every advantage to the favored group and none to the other group. Jealousy developed.

The Hutus living in the north held all the power. They used the newspapers and the radio to spark ethnic conflict. The Tutsis felt banished, and disorder came quickly.

First there were isolated episodes. In the beginning of 1992, Tutsis as well as Hutus from the south were killed in public. The killings happened quickly, for a week or ten days. Then they stopped.

I had just published my first report about human rights violations in Rwanda and organized a week of events devoted to respect for human rights. I was also organizing the first international mission of nongovernmental organizations [known as NGOs] to investigate human rights violations in Rwanda.

The authorities wanted to break me. They wanted the information that I was going to give to the international commission. They searched my office and my house and didn't find anything. So they made the big decision to kill me.

On December 22, 1992, I was riding in a cab. (In Rwanda you sit next to the taxi driver in the front seat.) My taxi driver drove so that the passenger side hit the phone pole. I went through the window. I still have the scars on my face. As soon as I left the hospital, I went right back to work.

After that there were other incidents. My vehicle was attacked, and it was only because I had a great driver that I was able to get out of that situation. I had no bodyguards. No gun. No machete. I decided that if they wanted to kill me they could do it whether I had guards or not. Besides, the guards would have been killed, too. The fact that I continued to work made the authorities afraid. They thought I was protected somehow. One official even thought that I was protected by the CIA.

When the genocide was about to begin, I faxed my partners

around the world. I faxed everyone I could think of. But the situation in Rwanda was rather strange. One day we thought this was it, everything was going to blow up. The next day everything was more or less calm, and we thought, Maybe it's going to be okay. Children were going to school. Markets were full. Life was ordinary.

On the night of the sixth of April, I had just written a fax to the Human Rights Watch office in New York. I told them that the people were arming themselves, the militia was walking around the streets with arms. "The situation here is very bad. A catastrophe is brewing."

That night, the plane carrying President Juvenal Habyarimana, a Hutu, crashed. The president and the new president of neighboring Burundi, who was flying with him, were killed. That detonated everything. Within ten minutes of the downing of the plane, barricades were in the roads. And within one hour, slaughters were being carried out as far away as sixty kilometers from the capital.

In so-called revenge, the military and the president's personal guard [the Presidential Guard] left their barracks and started killing people. They started killing everybody who was Tutsi, everybody who was from the south, and the intellectuals.

This was not anarchy. This was planned slaughter. There was absolutely no doubt not only that this was something that had been organized, but that the downing of the plane was part of the plan.

The Presidential Guard knew exactly which houses to visit. Among the people who were targeted to be assassinated were human rights activists. I called U.N. peacekeeping headquar-

ters [twenty-five hundred U.N. soldiers had been based in the capital] twenty-seven times to ask them to come and take me out of my neighborhood, which was being systematically decimated by the army. I called various embassies, but everyone was too busy to come and get me. There was no way that I could leave alone.

The killers had maps of each area. They went from house to house. It was planned and it was organized. When they came to my house, I was on the phone with Alison. [Alison Des Forges, a founding member of Human Rights Watch/Africa, is the principal point person in Rwanda.]

Alison is my sister. My twin sister. My white, American twin sister. I saw the military coming up my walk with their guns steaming because they had just killed someone. It was raining a little and the guns were steaming in the mist. I said to Alison, "They are here. This is the end. Please take care of my children."

Alison screamed, "Please stay on the line. *Stay on the line.*"

I said, "I don't want you to hear this," and I hung up the phone. Instinctively, I ran outside and hid myself in the bushes in back of the house. The soldiers asked the domestic help to open all the rooms. They looked for me everywhere. They went to every room, asking where I was.

Then there was an attack by the RPF [the Tutsi Rwandan Patriotic Front] on the outskirts of the city, and the military began to flee. They passed right by where I was hiding and continued on. When one soldier went around the house, another said to him, "I didn't hear you shoot, and you didn't bring her with you. Did she give you money?" The first one said, "No, go and look yourself. The domestic said she is not in Rwanda anymore. She lives in Europe now."

When the soldiers left, I went back into the house and hid in the eaves of the roof under the ceiling. I stayed there for a week.

It was too dangerous to come down and call Alison. She called my home a number of times, pretty much to verify that I was dead. She thought I was probably dead, but she wanted proof. When my domestic answered the phone, he said that I was in the sky. Alison was certain that meant that I was dead.

"No, no, the sky, the sky. She is not dead," he insisted. Alison didn't believe him.

Alison said, "If you can talk to her, go ask Monique who is the director of Africa Watch."

He climbed up to the rafters and asked me for the name. I said, "Abdullahi An-Na'im." Because Muslim names are not common in Rwanda, my domestic couldn't pronounce it properly and Alison still did not believe him. I had to climb down and tell Alison that I was alive.

A week later, I was finally able to leave, but it cost me all my money. The military from the Presidential Guard, who were doing the most killing, had left the area. The soldiers who stood guard in front of my house seemed very young and inexperienced. I put on my best clothes, marched outside, and demanded that they take me to a hotel.

Fortunately, the soldiers didn't recognize me as an activist. I took the precaution of bringing some photos of my ex-husband, a military man, with his friends, who were high-ranking officers.

Because nothing is free in Rwanda, the young soldiers asked for money. I gave them about $1,200 U.S. to take me eight kilometers to the hotel. A very expensive taxi. On the way, they stole everything else that I had, including Alison's mother's antique brooch, which I wore last year when I met President Clinton at the White House. I was particularly upset about losing that brooch. But they did take me to the hotel and did not harm me.

At the hotel, the soldiers said that they were going to come back. They thought that I could get them more money. I didn't worry about that. There were other things to worry about.

The first thing I did was call Alison to tell her that I arrived at the hotel safely. I apologized for waking her up so early in the morning, four A.M., New York time. Although I was the one who was there physically, I did not suffer alone. My friends suffered with me. Alison told me that when she thought that I was dead, she died, too.

Alison telephoned our friends in Belgium, Canada, and at the United Nations. She asked that they arrange for my evacuation. The Belgians were the last ones to be evacuated from Rwanda, and Alison asked them to take me with them.

The next day, when I called the Belgians, everything was arranged. I asked the consul to pick me up at the hotel. He could not. The battle for Kigali was beginning; they had already lost lots of Belgian soldiers and could not risk any more lives. It was up to me to find my own way.

I ran into an old Canadian missionary and asked him to take me to the place where the Belgians were assembling to be evacuated, about one and a half kilometers away. In those dark days in Kigali, that was a long, long way. He said that he would do it but his car didn't have gas. I looked around the hotel and found a Rwandan businessman whom I could trust. As a young politician, he had problems himself. He also was persecuted. Most important, he had a car and the car had gas.

I said, "Come on, let's go! We're going to have an adventure. We're going to try to get ourselves evacuated by the Belgians."

"Maybe the Belgians will take you, but they are not going to take me," he told me.

"Listen, if they take me, they're going to take you. If they don't take you, they're not going to take me, either." The three of us—the Canadian missionary, the politician, and I—were on our way.

A new problem arose. We hit a roadblock filled with drunken soldiers. They decided to kill us. Just as the guns were pointed at our heads, one of the young soldiers recognized the old missionary. The soldier had been a student at the mission where the Canadian taught. That saved us. We continued down the road without any further problems.

The politician was correct. The Belgians did agree to take me out of the country, but they refused to take him. To make them take him, too, I pretended that he was my husband. The Belgian diplomat knew me and laughed. "But, Monique, you're not married."

"Oh, yes, I got married two days ago," I said.

The Belgian guy said, "How can you have gotten married? There is a war going on."

I told him, "For a marriage you need two people. A woman and a man. *Voilà*. There is the man. I am the woman. Did this man tell you that he was not my husband? He's my husband and I'm taking him with me." I refused to budge.

A Swiss diplomat was awaiting evacuation as well. He said to the Belgian, "Listen, don't complicate this any further. You have an order from the prime minister to evacuate this woman from Rwanda. The prime minister will understand if you evacuate this woman with her husband. The prime minister is not going to understand if you refuse to evacuate her because she has a husband."

We flew to Belgium, and then I went on to New York, where I was reunited with my friends at Human Rights Watch. I was surprised that I was still alive.

A Message from Monique:

Human rights work is a personal involvement. If each person decides to save one other person, there will be no more human rights violations.

Monique and Alison reunited

III
The Right to One's Life

Every human being has the inherent right to life. This
right shall be protected by law. No one shall be arbi-
trarily deprived of his life.

International Covenant
on Civil and Political Rights
Article 6, 1

CHAPTER 5

Final Justice

BRIEFING—BRAZIL

At one o'clock in the morning of July 25, 1993, two cars drove into a fancy tourist area near the Candelária Cathedral in Rio de Janeiro, Brazil. Men dressed in plain clothes approached a group of teenage boys who were living and sleeping on the street. They asked to see the leader of the gang, a boy known as Ruço.

Earlier the gang of boys had been involved in an argument with police, who had tried to confiscate glue that they were sniffing. When the argument escalated, some boys threw rocks at a police van, breaking a window. A policeman promised to return and "take care of this."

The kids said that they didn't know where Ruço was. They were lying, of course. He was actually right there with them. The men pulled out guns and opened fire. Four boys were killed instantly. A fifth boy stumbled a few blocks and died in

94

Burial of street child

front of the Candelária Cathedral. The sixth boy, Ruço, died several days later from gunshot wounds to his right eye and thigh.

After the initial killings, the men stopped three other boys several blocks away, shot them, and dumped their bodies at the Museum of Modern Art. One of the three boys survived. The killings of the eight street children in Rio de Janeiro became known as the "Candelária Massacre."

This incident, widely reported in the press, generated a wave of indignation and shock in Brazil and abroad. To the credit of the Rio authorities, several of the men were arrested. There was an investigation, and three policemen were indicted. According to Human Rights Watch, "with the exception of the public outcry and the hastily taken reforms, the Candelária

killings reflect a consistent pattern investigated by Americas Watch during the month spent in Brazil researching homicides of children. Though the Candelária killing was uncommon because of the number of children killed at once, it was far from an unusual occurrence. According to the Ministério Público, between 1988 and 1991, a total of 5,644 children from the ages of five to seventeen were victims of violent deaths. In the state of Rio de Janeiro alone, according to figures from the state civil police, 424 children under the age of eighteen were victims of homicide in 1992, and 298 were killed in the first six months of 1993. As in the Candelária case, many of the victims are minors who sleep and work on the streets of Brazil's cities. The majority of the victims are male and aged fourteen to seventeen, and a disproportionate share is black."[1]

Ben Penglase, a twenty-six-year-old U.S. research associate for Human Rights Watch/Americas, hoped someday to research human rights problems in Brazil. Soon after the Candelária Massacre, he got his chance.

Ben Penglase
Researcher for Human Rights Watch/Americas

As an American kid growing up in Brazil, I was very much aware of the differences between those with incredible wealth and those in incredible poverty. In Rio, shantytowns were put up near the wealthy parts of the city. I grew up in Rio de Janeiro because my dad worked for Exxon Oil in Brazil and Latin America. Even though I went to a private American school, I became fluent in Portuguese.

I'd often play soccer on the beach with very poor kids who lived in the neighborhood. It was easily apparent that those kids' lives were remarkably different from mine. Some lived in houses without electricity. Others lived in cardboard boxes in areas that had open sewers. Most didn't own much more than the shorts and sandals they were wearing. They couldn't read or write very well. Many came from horribly violent family situations. Like most kids our age, we had common interests: playing soccer, hanging out at the beach, and having fun.

When I reached college age, I returned to the States, where I attended Stanford University, majoring in international relations. I focused on Brazil and Latin America, with a side interest in South Africa.

After college I got a job at Human Rights Watch as an entry-level administrative person. I helped with mailings, answered phones, all that sort of stuff. Then the woman who was doing our Brazilian research on rural labor problems wasn't able to finish her project because she was needed in Kurdistan. The organization desperately needed a Portuguese-speaking person to finish the research. I suppose I was in the right place at the right time.

In June 1993, a colleague and I were sent to Brazil to investigate the problems of violence against adolescents. We decided to look into this problem, because from the stories that we read in the press we got the impression that there were death squads running around the streets of Brazil killing any kid they found. Much of the reporting was sensationalism.

Our job was to observe the human rights abuses against

children in Brazil, analyze what was causing it, and then examine the government's response. If there were positive things that the government was doing, it deserved international recognition. If there were negative things that the government was doing, it needed to be loudly criticized.

RETURN TO BRAZIL

My return to Brazil was very depressing. With Brazil's recent return to democracy [there was a military dictatorship from 1964 until about 1988], the people could now elect their governors and state representatives. The press could say virtually anything it wanted without worrying about being censored by the government. But at the same time, violence had become worse, and the police force that had committed horrible crimes during the military rule was even more out of control. It was especially depressing because so many of the problems were rooted in poverty and social inequality.

When we arrived in Rio, I met with street educators, a Brazilian version of social workers. These educators work with groups of kids who live in the streets. They teach them how to read, give out information about health and sexual diseases, and try to get them into drug treatment programs. Some of the people I met were truly inspirational. Gecivaldo Barbosa Alves, a twenty-six-year-old street educator, has been running a home for boys and girls for eight years. His group included seven adolescent boys and six adolescent girls. Some of these kids had left their houses because they were the victims of child abuse. Often the mother had taken up with a stepfather who would get drunk and beat the boys or sexually abuse the girls. Some of the kids had been sent out to sell newspapers, wash cars, or do *anything* to bring in income. Usually they ended up dealing drugs. The longer they stayed on the streets, the more likely they were to lose contact with their families. I interviewed many of the kids who lived with Gecivaldo.

I also talked to other kids living in shelters. They told me about their experiences with the police and about violence done against them. I needed to know as many details as possible. The kids had no problem when I wrote things down, but when I taped them, they clammed up. Some of the adolescent boys were embarrassed to tell me that somebody beat them up. Other kids were afraid for their safety. I eventually got them to open up by explaining that if I could present their stories, maybe it would help other kids.

Shop owners and folks who lived in the neighborhood felt threatened by the street kids. They did not believe that the Brazilian justice system could take care of their problems. And to a certain extent, they were right. The Brazilian justice system is pretty hopeless at actually investigating crimes and convicting people. The shop owners felt that they must deal with the problem of potential thieves on their own. So they hired somebody, maybe an off-duty policeman, to get rid of the kids.

There's no way that the police can guard all the neighborhoods, all the streets. They are limited to inefficient patrols. Meanwhile, crime increases and the criminals multiply. If it weren't for us, the Baixada [an urban area north of Rio] wouldn't be safe. There would be waves of mugging, looting, and invasions of homes all the time. We impose respect. Where

we act, the bandits can't be lazy. They know that if
they mess around, they're dead.

> Statement made by "Marreco," a former
> policeman and a confessed member
> of the *Justiça Final* (Final Justice),
> a Rio de Janeiro death squad.[2]

At least initially, organized vigilantes sometimes provide security and protection for a neighborhood. Neighborhood folks hire these guys to scare off potential thieves. But what often happens is that the vigilantes themselves get involved in the crime. Some death squads give the impression that they are providing law and order, but often they themselves are the organized criminals.

There are some people within the Rio police force who make an effort to investigate these problems. But at the same time, there is a high level of corruption of street-level police officers by organized crime. Many of the commanders are aware of what is going on, but do nothing to stop it.

EDSON DAMIÃO CALIXTO

The most troubling were the cases of kids who had survived assassination attempts. In a northeastern city of Brazil, we investigated the case of Edson Damião Calixto, a fourteen-year-old boy who had been abandoned at an early age. Edson lived in a very poor neighborhood and worked in a junkyard. One night in 1991, he was walking down a road when a boy ran up to him, gave him a paper bag, and said, "Hang on to this." The boy then ran into the woods. A few minutes later a police van showed up and asked Edson what was in the paper bag. When he opened the bag, he found a loaded .38 revolver. The police took the gun, beat him up, made him lie down on the ground, put a gun to the back of his head, and accused him of being a neighborhood thief. They wanted to know where he was keeping the money and the objects he had stolen. He denied having done any of this. They handcuffed him, put him in the back of the police van, drove him around the neighborhood, stopped at a few houses in the neighborhood, and boasted that they had captured the thief and were going to take care of him if he didn't admit to the crimes he'd committed.

Eventually, they drove him to a vacant lot on the outskirts of the city, tied a T-shirt around his head, had him kneel down in front of a wall, and shot him in the back several times. Miraculously, he survived. He lay on the ground, pretending to be dead, and eventually passed out from loss of blood. A few hours later he awoke and realized that he could move around a little bit. He could lift up his hands but he couldn't move much more than that. A car was coming toward him, so he waved to it, hoping that the driver would take him to the hospital.

The car turned out to contain the very police who were returning to make certain that Edson was dead. When they realized that he was alive, they put him back in the car, drove to a trash heap on the outskirts of town, and shot him one more time.

Still, Edson survived. By now, he was too terrified to flag down another car. Somehow he managed to crawl to the side of the road. The following morning, people who lived nearby found him and took him to the hospital. He's now paralyzed from the waist down.

My colleague interviewed Edson in the hospital. His story was really heartbreaking. Here was this fourteen-year-old kid who couldn't understand why this was happening. "Why me? Why did they grab me? Why did they shoot me? I haven't done anything wrong," he asked. What kind of answer can you give?

Some of the kids were very angry, and others were simply resigned. Many had come to accept this level of violence in their lives as normal. In fact, many kids didn't see anything unusual about being beaten by the police or having their friends killed. For them, that was their daily life. They said that there was no point in complaining about it because nothing would ever be done to make it better.

Not all the kids were totally innocent victims. I talked to one boy who boasted about all the crimes he had committed. He talked about holding people up at gunpoint. He was proud of his crimes. But should this boy be hunted down and killed? Certainly, even kids who are committing crimes don't deserve that kind of treatment.

The kids being killed were mainly poor, black or dark-skinned adolescent boys, aged fifteen to seventeen. A significant number of them may have been involved in drug dealing or petty theft. There is a lot of police participation in these crimes. At one point, I asked a boy if the police needed them as informants, and he said, "Why do they need informants? They are the ones who are running everything." Kids were blackmailed by the police because they were dealing drugs, because they were thieves, or simply because they were poor, uneducated, and unable to defend themselves. More often than not, a kid was killed because he was involved with corrupt policemen, he failed to pay off policemen, or he was seen as a menace in the neighborhood. Some kids were involved in a drug transaction that went bad. Many were simply caught in the cross fire or mistaken for somebody else.

On one hand, it was hard to tell with complete precision whether or not these kids were telling the truth. Most of them didn't want their real names used, and that made it difficult to get the police version of the event. On the other hand, the sheer quantity of events with so many common factors made it very unlikely that they were making this up. Local human rights organizations had documented similar patterns.

SYSTEM OF JUSTICE

Often the police claimed that they had come upon the scene of a crime and the kids shot at them. Then they fired back. When I looked at these cases closely and interviewed witnesses, it became apparent that instead of arresting a kid, the police just shot him. The police believed that the justice system was so messed up that if they arrested the kid, he would never be sentenced and he'd end up right back on the streets.

In one unusual case, one of the policemen was actually convicted, a very, very rare event. Enéas da Silva was a poor, black, sixteen-year-old boy who lived on the outskirts of São Paulo in a shantytown. One evening he was sitting outside with a group of friends, reading a pornographic magazine. When the kids saw a police car come around the corner, they took off. Enéas ran into an alley. The policemen pulled up in their car, jumped out with their loaded revolvers, and went after him. The neighbors heard him pleading for his life, saying, "Don't shoot me. I'm not a bandit." One policeman shot him twice in cold blood.

Then, to make it seem like a shoot-out, they fired their guns into the air, ran back to their police car, and asked for backup. Enéas was already dead. Various neighbors heard him being shot and witnessed what had happened. Then the police planted a gun next to his right hand. Later it was discovered that Enéas was left-handed. He was an average kid, not known to be involved in crime. Even though he was already dead, the police put him into the police car and drove him to the hospital. This is another thing that they frequently do so that they can claim that they tried to rescue the child.

This was a very rare case, because one of the policemen involved, the guy who actually pulled the trigger, was convicted and sentenced to two years in prison. The vast majority of these cases either never come to trial—there have been cases that have been under investigation for ten or fifteen years—or when they do come to trial, the policeman says, "Look, it was self-defense. I shot this kid in a shoot-out." In this instance the conviction came about because human rights groups in Brazil were following the case very closely and did a terrific job making sure the witnesses were heard in court. Local human rights groups helped arrange for their protection and, in some circumstances, moved witnesses to other cities. Although the witnesses were afraid for their lives, they courageously testified and the policeman was convicted. It's a hopeful sign.

After talking to the kids, I spoke with the police to get their version of events. Brazil is a lot like the United States in that the state governments are relatively powerful. The governor controls the state's police force except for a federal force, which is kind of like the FBI in the States.

The police made it difficult for me to do my job. They'd refuse to meet with me, not show up when they said they would, not have the information that they said they'd have. Actually, the kids often did the same thing.

I don't think I was ever in danger. I hope not. I think that the police were smart enough to know that doing anything to me would cause a lot more problems for them. It would generate a lot more publicity for them because I was a researcher for a human rights organization.

I named my report "Final Justice" because it was the name of a death squad in a poor neighborhood in Rio de Janeiro. (The guy who runs it is apparently a former policeman who was kicked off the police force because of involvement in corruption.) Death squads in Brazil often see themselves as taking care of crime in a situation where the government can't do so. Very, very frequently these squads are made up of uniformed police who patrol the neighborhoods in the daytime and then moonlight after work. They take their uniforms off and become the death squads. I couldn't interview any of them. I wanted to. I tried to get into a prison to interview someone who actually had been arrested, but the authorities wouldn't give me permission.

Actually, and this is very Brazilian, an official would say to me, "Look, I know that we have this problem. It is really terrible but, you know, we have police that don't get paid very much. We're trying our best to make sure they are not corrupt, but things happen. We assure you that we are doing everything we can to investigate these instances and to prosecute these people."

For me, the most rewarding part is working with human rights activists in other countries who, often at personal risk, have devoted their lives to making a difference. They are the real heroes of human rights.

A MESSAGE FROM BEN:

In many ways teaching school, being a social worker, working in a legal aid clinic, or teaching in an English-as-a-second language program is a far more direct way of improving people's human rights. What ultimately counts most is an honest attempt to help each other.

Chapter 6

Cruel and Unusual Punishment

BRIEFING—THE UNITED STATES

In 1882, Thomas Edison astonished the entire world when he lit up Wall Street. His only problem was that the voltage from the direct current (DC) that he used was too low to travel more than about a mile from its power station. George Westinghouse, a competitor of Edison, solved the voltage problem by using alternating current (AC) to transmit electricity more powerfully. Thus began the "battle of the currents."

Edison wanted to convince the public that Westinghouse's AC current was more dangerous than his own, and he came up with an unusual idea. In courts and laboratories in the United States, the "science of death" was being studied in order to find a humane and speedy way to carry out capital punishment. Hanging was often bungled, the guillotine was too bloody, and shooting was considered offensive (except in the military). A new method of death—electrocution—became the method of choice. According to the Supreme Court, electro-cution was "a step forward . . . based on grounds of mercy and humanity."

Even though he himself was opposed to capital punishment, Edison lobbied passionately for the electric chair. He said that "an electric current of 1,000 volts would kill instantly, pain-lessly, and in every case." And he endorsed the use of AC [West-inghouse's current] because his own DC "doesn't seem to have much effect on the nerves."

Edison reasoned that if AC were used to kill people in the electric chair, Americans would never allow it into their homes to cook their meals and light their rooms. "The executioner's current," he called it. Westinghouse was furious.

At about this time, William Kemmler, an ax murderer from Buffalo, was the first person to be sentenced to death by elec-trocution. Westinghouse paid for Kemmler's appeal and fought his execution all the way to the Supreme Court. In spite of Westinghouse's hard work to save Kemmler—and his AC current—the execution went ahead as scheduled.

Edison personally showed the authorities how to wire the pair of generators used in the execution. Current passed through Kemmler's body for seventeen seconds. To the horror of the witnesses, Kemmler was still breathing. The executioners used a second jolt, which continued for about four minutes. (Officially it was reported as lasting a minute and a half.) Wit-nesses reported a "terrible stench of burning flesh and singed hair filling the room" as Kemmler literally "roasted to death."

This hideous scene proved too much for some of the wit-nesses. Even the district attorney who prosecuted the case "bolted from the room and collapsed in the hall."[1]

Today many states are switching to a new "humane" method of death: lethal injection. Is it humane? The Reverend Joseph B. Ingle, of the United Church of Christ, does not think so. Joe is a minister to death row inmates.

Joe Ingle
Activist / Minister—The United States

I will be very candid with you. In the United States, the attempt to abolish the death penalty is a losing proposition. All the polls reflect popular support for the death penalty. In part, that's because we have no political leadership on this issue. In another part, it's the strong opinion of the white majority, which is fueled by their fear of crime. We're quite willing to dispatch human beings if it will give us some sense of protection. As a result, it is hard for Americans to see the death penalty as a human rights issue. But it clearly is.

> *At the highest level in the international community, the United Nations has steadily moved from a neutral position to an abolitionist one. In numerous documents, the United Nations has deemed the death penalty to be a violation of the fundamental right to life, and to be "cruel, inhuman or degrading punishment."[2]*

I want to give an overview of the death penalty in the United States to provide a basic framework for the problems. In 1972, the United States Supreme Court struck down the death pen-

alty throughout the United States. The court declared it randomly and freakishly imposed against black people in particular. That case was called *Furman v. Georgia*. Four years later, in 1976, the same U.S. Supreme Court reinstated the death penalty in a series of decisions. *(Gregg v. Georgia; Proffitt v. Florida; Jurek v. Texas)*. Executions began again, in January of 1977, with the death of Gary Gilmore in the state of Utah.

> *Gary Gilmore's case was portrayed in the book,* The Executioner's Song, *by Norman Mailer. Gilmore elected to be killed by firing squad. When his request was granted, Supreme Court Justice Thurgood Marshall called the execution "state-administered suicide."*

Today in the United States there are more than three thousand people on death row. We call the South, where I come from, the "death belt." That is because we have more people on death row and we execute more people than any other region of the country. Why do we do this in the South? you may wonder. Is the South so vengeful?

We do it because of race. The death penalty is an institution driven by the fears of the white majority and directed against people who are convicted of killing white people.

Let me give you a test. Tell me the number of white people who have been executed for killing a black person. Here's a clue: We've had 18,804 executions since 1608, the date of the first execution in what is today the United States.

The answer? Thirty-one. We really can't even say thirty-one, because ten of these were white people executed under the laws of the day because they destroyed their property: slaves.

We are a very violent country. In 1994 in the United States

we had approximately 24,000 murders. As a result of those 24,000 murders around 200 prisoners ended up on death row. Who are these 200 people? Are they the people who commit the most heinous crimes? No, in many cases, they are not.

> *In countries which have not abolished the death penalty, sentence of death may be imposed only for the most serious crimes in accordance with the law in force at the time of the commission of the crime and not contrary to the provisions of the present Covenant and to the Convention on the Prevention and Punishment of the Crime of Genocide. This penalty can only be carried out pursuant to a final judgment rendered by a competent court.*
>
> International Covenant
> on Civil and Political Rights

The two characteristics that you find again and again when you visit death row, and I've been visiting men and women on death row in the South for twenty years, are: one, a person is convicted of killing a white person; and two, the convicted person is poor.

So we have two factors: race and economics. Nine out of ten people facing the death penalty in the United States cannot afford a lawyer. And that means they get a court-appointed defender who, more often than not, does not know anything about the death penalty issues or how to defend anyone facing the death penalty.

The incidence of murder is very high in the African-American community. It is primarily black-on-black crime. These criminals hardly ever get the death penalty. Another way to see the discrimination at work is by recognizing that 45 percent of the people on death row are African-Americans, even though they make up only 12 percent of the population.

As reported in the 1987 Supreme Court case of *McCleskey v. Kemp,* the defendant, McCleskey,

> *proffered a statistical study performed by Professors David C. Baldus, Charles Pulaski, and George Woodworth (the Baldus study) that purports to show a disparity in the imposition of the death sentence in Georgia based on the race of the murder victim and, to a lesser extent, the race of the defendant. The Baldus study is actually two sophisticated statistical studies that examine over 2,000 murder cases that occurred in Georgia during the 1970s. The raw numbers collected by Professor Baldus indicate that defendants charged with killing white persons received the death penalty in 11 percent of the cases, but defendants charged with killing blacks received the death penalty in only 1 percent of the cases. . . . One of his models concludes that, even after taking account of 39 nonracial variables, defendants charged with killing white victims were 4.3 times as likely to receive a death sentence as defendants charged with killing blacks.[3]*

WILLIE DARDEN

I'd like to tell you about a man named Willie Darden. I got to know Willie in the Florida State Prison. Willie and I called each other "homeboy" because we were from the same part of

North Carolina. Willie was born and raised in North Carolina, one county over from mine. North Carolina was a segregated state when I was growing up, and we never knew each other.

Willie grew up on a farm that had been leased to his grandfather. When Willie was ten years old, his grandfather died and his stepmother deserted the family. Willie dropped out of school to work the farm and care for his brothers and sisters. When he turned sixteen, he stole forty dollars from the mailbox of a white man. For that crime, the state of North Carolina sent him to the Training School for Boys, a segregated juvenile facility, for four years. When Willie got out of prison, he returned to eastern North Carolina, but he couldn't really make a living. He started drifting around the South. By 1974 he had ended up in Lakeland, Florida.

One evening, at about five-thirty, a young black man walked into Turman's Furniture Store in Lakeland. He held it up and shot and killed Mr. Turman. A neighbor, a teenage boy, heard the shooting and ran in just as the robber was leaving the store. The robber wounded the teenager and then fled into the night in a green car.

What Willie Darden had in common with the person who robbed and killed Mr. Turman was that he was black, he was a stranger, and he drove a green car. The police picked Willie up. This is how they ID'd him: They put Willie in a small room and brought in the victim's wife, who had been standing next to her husband when he had been shot. Willie Darden, the only black person in the room, was sitting in a chair. The district attorney asked, "Is this the man who killed your husband?"

She said, "I guess so."

Then they took a series of photographs of Willie and took them to the teenage boy who was in the hospital. They showed the boy photographs of three different black men. Only one of them was wearing a little sign that said "Bartow County Jail." That was around Willie Darden's neck.

"Who committed this crime?" they asked. The young boy in the hospital looked at the photographs and picked out Willie Darden.

That was the evidence that brought Willie to trial. As Willie later told me, when he walked into the courtroom, he knew what was going to happen. The entire courtroom was filled with white people. A white jury. White prosecutor. White judge. White defense attorney. White everybody, except Willie.

In the closing argument, the prosecutor pointed to Willie and said, "Willie Darden is an animal who should be placed on a leash. . . . [He] should be sitting here with no face, blown away by a shotgun." He inflamed the jury with his remarks.

The prosecutor should not use arguments calculated to inflame the passions or prejudices of the jury.
ABA Standards for Criminal Justice

The jury brought back the death verdict and Governor Bob Graham signed Willie's death warrant. (While he was governor, Graham signed 155 death warrants that resulted in the deaths of eighteen people.)

Willie's death sentence brought him to Florida's prison, and that's where I met him. He was on death row from 1974 to 1988. He was called the "dean of death row" because he was there for so long.

Willie Darden

As his case proceeded, we found some good lawyers to argue his appeal. They investigated his case and found a woman, Christine Bass, who gave evidence through an affidavit about the night of the murder. Bass said that Willie Darden was in her house between four in the afternoon and five-thirty. His car had broken down in front of her house, and he had come inside to call a wrecker. There was no way he could have driven across town in time to rob and shoot Mr. Turman.

We were able to submit Christine Bass's affidavit to the

court, but we were not able to have an evidentiary hearing. In an evidentiary hearing, we would have been able to bring Christine Bass herself forward as a witness.

After several stays of execution as Willie's case traveled through the court system, it was brought before the Supreme Court in September 1986. The Court refused to hear our argument. The execution was to proceed on schedule.

On the night of the execution, I went into the prison with Willie's sweetheart, Felicia, for a last visit. We were there from seven until midnight. Willie was to be executed at dawn.

At midnight, Felicia's visit was just about over. I sat down in a chair while Willie said good-bye to her. Afterward, I planned to go back to Willie's cell and minister to him throughout the night.

All of a sudden I heard shouting. I looked up and saw one of my colleagues running down the corridor, screaming. "We have a stay! We have a stay of execution!"

How did this happen? In the United States Supreme Court, it takes four votes for the Court to decide to hear a case, but it takes five votes to grant a stay of execution. Earlier, we lost the stay by a five-to-four vote. That meant that four justices wanted to hear the case. But we needed five votes for a stay of execution. Sometime between five P.M. and midnight, Justice Lewis Franklin Powell, Jr., changed his vote.

Willie's execution was stayed, and later in 1987 his case came up before the Supreme Court. It was argued by his lawyers. The Court made its decision. Willie lost.

In the dissenting opinion, Justice Blackmun wrote . . . "I cannot conclude that McDaniel's [the prosecutor] sustained assault on Darden's very humanity did not affect the jury's ability to judge the credibility questioned on the real evidence before it. Because I believe that he did not have a trial that was fair, I would reverse Darden's conviction; I would not allow him to go to his death until he has been convicted at a fair trial.

"Twice during the past year—in United States v. Young *and again today—this Court has been faced with clearly improper prosecutorial misconduct during summations. Each time, the Court has condemned the behavior but affirmed the conviction. . . ."*[4]

The new execution date was set for the spring of 1988. That spring was a very happy time in my life because my wife and I were about to adopt a child. Our daughter was born March 5. On March 8, I learned that Willie's execution date had been set for March 15.

Willie had his lawyers call me and say: "Joe, don't come down here. Stay at home with your wife and your new baby."

How could I? I went back to Florida on March 13 to be with Willie. We repeated the same scenario that we had gone through two years before: Felicia went in to see him. We stayed till midnight. When the clock struck twelve, she got to hug Willie one time. No kissing allowed. One final hug.

The execution was set for seven A.M. Felicia left in tears; I went with Willie back to his cell. I sat outside Willie's cell and talked with him all night through the cell bars. We went through his mail. He had hundreds of letters from all over the world from people who had heard about his case. Even Andrei Sakharov, the Russian dissident and Nobel Prize recipient, had written to the governor asking him to stop the execution. The governor would not do it.

Willie was held in the basement of the prison. The windows were high up. Toward the end of the night, I looked up and saw it was beginning to get a little light outside. Dawn was breaking. The death squad would come soon to take Willie to the electric chair.

I had smuggled two cigars into the area, and we smoked them together. It was time to say good-bye. He asked me to witness his execution. Now, my cardinal rule in doing this work is not to witness an execution. I had worked for years with twenty people who had been executed. I had come to love them and care for them. And to watch someone execute them . . . I just wouldn't do it.

But I had known Willie for ten years. I was his homeboy. I told him that I would be there. We said good-bye. The death squad came to get him, and I moved into a surrealistic world within the Florida State Prison. At six A.M., all the witnesses to the execution were taken to a room where we were given breakfast. Hanging on one wall was the United States flag and the State of Florida flag. On the Florida flag was inscribed, "In God We Trust." I sat there, drinking orange juice and staring at those flags.

After breakfast, we were driven in two white vans to the execution chamber, at the tip of the prison. We went into the witness part of the death chamber. The electric chair was right in front of us. At 6:58, two minutes before seven o'clock, they brought Willie through the door. He came in erect, proud. He looked like an African king. His head was shaved, along with a spot on his right leg, so that the electricity could better go through his body.

They put him in this chair and they strapped his legs down. They strapped his arms and they strapped his chest. They placed a microphone beside him in case he wanted to make a last statement.

Willie proceeded to give the most eloquent statement of his innocence. He talked about his appreciation for the people who had worked with him over the years to try to save his life. He did this while sitting, strapped down, in the electric chair.

I was standing at the rear of the witness room of the execution chamber so that Willie could see me easily. When he finished his statement, he looked at me and he winked, just to let me know that he knew that I was there and appreciated it. They dropped a black mask over his face. Just before they electrocuted him, he waved good-bye to me with his left hand.

They ran 2,400 volts of electricity through his body and he was pronounced dead by the doctors at twelve minutes after seven. I went to be with Felicia, the woman who loved him, to try to comfort her.

The man was totally innocent.

THE POLITICS OF DEATH

Another person I worked with was Velma Barfield, of North Carolina. So far, Velma is the only woman executed in the United States since the death penalty was reestablished in 1976.

Velma grew up very poor in eastern North Carolina. She

worked all her life. I got to know her when she was a fifty-three-year-old grandmother on death row at the women's prison in Raleigh, North Carolina. She was plump, kind, and had a sunny disposition. Velma was beloved by the other prisoners and by the guards. Virginia Lancaster, the warden, loved Velma Barfield.

It was hard to reconcile the fact that this delightful person whom I was visiting had freely confessed to murdering four people, including her husband. How could this be possible? I couldn't bring these concepts together.

I found a lawyer for her after her case went up on appeal. He took this case pro bono [no fee]. We discovered that Velma had suffered extensive physical and sexual abuse from her father and her older brother. As a result of this abuse, Velma would have periodic bouts of depression. She went to a doctor who prescribed a drug that precipitated a bipolar mood disorder. She became psychotic. When she was in this psychotic state, she'd put rat poison in the food of people she loved. No one had discovered this fact until our psychiatrist evaluated her and found this out. No court had ever asked these questions.

We took this information to Governor Jim Hunt of North Carolina. It would be his decision whether to give Velma clemency and commute her sentence to life in prison, or to allow the execution to proceed. Jim Hunt was running for a U.S. Senate seat against Jesse Helms. The election was set for November 6, 1984. Velma Barfield's execution date was set for November 2, 1984. We met with Governor Hunt in September 1984 to ask for clemency. He was very formal, very cold. He made no commitment. Later, Warden Lancaster made a private appointment with the governor to beg for Velma Barfield's life.

On September 28, 1984, Governor Hunt held a press conference and denied clemency for Velma Barfield. He made statements to the effect that Velma enjoyed watching her victims die. What Governor Hunt did at that press conference is what we call "the politics of death." The issue of the death penalty is used as a vehicle to promote political careers. In this case, it was Governor Hunt's career.

We went back to court one final time with the new information that the prescription drugs sent Velma into a psychotic state, and therefore that she was not guilty by reason of insanity. We went through three levels of courts in three days, trying to get a stay of execution.

On November 2, near two A.M., Velma Barfield was taken into the death chamber, strapped on a gurney. An I.V. was put into her arm. She was poisoned by lethal injection, which, by the way, is not a painless death. It's like being suffocated, like having a pillow put over your face. It's very, very painful.

Outside the prison during the execution, we held a protest vigil, and about one thousand people attended. Across the street were the celebrants, the people who cheered Velma Barfield's execution. When the execution was announced over a loudspeaker, the celebrants screamed, "Kill the bitch! Kill the bitch! Kill the bitch!"

All across the United States we are seeing politicians building their careers by killing citizens, which is what Governor Hunt thought he could do with Velma Barfield. (In fact, Jim Hunt lost the election. Perhaps the voters in North Carolina were appalled by his behavior.)

When people argue that those who commit violent crimes

must pay for them with their lives, I tell them about Velma Barfield. I tell them about Willie Darden. They're the reality. They're the ones who get caught in this net we throw out for people who can't afford a lawyer, for people who are not responsible for what they are doing, and for people who are accused and convicted of killing white people. It's not as simple as it is depicted in the newspapers and political speeches. It never is.

ABOUT JOE

If the truth be told, I came to this profession pretty much accidentally. I was born and raised in North Carolina. My childhood was typical for a white, lower-middle-class kid. I went to St. Andrews Presbyterian College and got an excellent education. In college I began thinking critically. I continued my studies at the Union Theological Seminary in New York City. While there, as part of the seminary's program, I lived and worked in East Harlem. Needless to say, I was in culture shock for a few months, but as I got to know the community, it became a wonderful experience. Interestingly, even though it was clear that I wasn't from around East Harlem, lots of my neighbors were black folks who came up from the South. They still had family there. My neighbors and I had a great deal in common. In East Harlem I learned about myself and about what it was like to be poor in an urban ghetto.

The seminary required that seniors do community work for twenty hours a week. In the fall of 1971, my senior year, I was in my apartment watching the Attica prison riots unfold on my fuzzy black-and-white TV.

Attica Prison is a maximum-security prison near Buffalo, New York. One thousand inmates seized control of the prison, demanding better living conditions. Negotiations broke down and state troopers stormed the prison. Ten hostages and thirty-one prisoners were killed, all by those who retook the prison. Later, a state commission found that the inmates had legitimate grievances.

I said to myself, "I'm going to spend my senior year visiting some people in a jail or a prison."

During that year I visited men at the Bronx House of Detention, just across the river from my home in East Harlem. I'd jump in my little Toyota and drive across the river into the Bronx House of D. It totally turned me around. Up until that time, I didn't have any notion of becoming a minister. I was interested in philosophy and religion.

Even though I'd gone through a training program, I had no idea what prison would be like. The first time I went to the prison, I took the elevator to the sixth floor and walked up to a barred door. I showed the guard my clergy badge, and he unlocked the door and escorted me in.

As soon as we stepped in, the guard locked the door behind us. Slam! We were in a walkway at the top of the cell block. The guard said, "People meet with their clients down here," and he gestured to a room at the end of the walk. As we were walking toward the room, we passed a door that led to the cell block. I said, "I'd like to be in there with the men."

This guy looked at me like, you gotta be kidding. He shrugged his shoulders and said, "Okay, if that's what you want to do. . . ." I don't know why I wanted to do that. I did know that I did not want to meet these guys in a cold, bare room. I wanted to meet them where they lived.

He unlocked that door and I stepped across the threshold. Then he slammed the door behind me and returned to his post. Once I stepped onto the walk, I noticed that all the individual cell doors were open. The first thing that flashed across my mind was, "Oh . . . my . . . God, he's locked me in here with these animals." I no sooner had this thought when the man in the first bunk looked up and said, "Man, what are *you* doing in here?"

"Well, I'm here to visit you guys this year," I replied. He introduced himself and invited me to sit down in his bunk. We talked. After a while he took me down the hall and introduced me to everybody on the walk. I felt like he was bringing me into his living room.

I liked all the people I worked with that year. I liked them a lot. But I will never forget that my knee-jerk reaction was what most other Americans' reaction is about people in prison. *Oh, my God, I'm locked in here with these animals.* That's the way we're socialized. That experience illustrates our perceptions of people in prison.

I spent a year visiting those men, who, with one exception, were black or Puerto Rican. They were locked up because they were poor and awaiting trial. If they had had money, they could have posted bond and gotten out. The average length of stay awaiting trial was about eighteen months. Some of the men appeared to be innocent.

There are way, way too many people locked up in this country. We should be involved in a whole different process of criminal justice. We should be trying to restore both the victim and the offender rather than just this retributive nonsense. It's a false premise to think that these people are irredeemable and should be thrown on a slag heap.

I decided that when I went back South, I would get involved in prison ministry. I moved to Nashville, Tennessee, and helped start the Southern Prison Ministry and later, the Southern Coalition on Jails and Prisons.

In 1976, when the Supreme Court reinstated the death penalty, we began a visitation program so that everybody on death row had a visitor from the outside. We recruited lawyers because many of these folks didn't have personal lawyers, only court-appointed ones.

Of the twenty people I worked with who've been executed, four of them were undoubtedly innocent. I'm not talking about cases where there was some possibility that the person might not be guilty. I'm talking about people whose innocence had been unmistakenly proven.

A Message from Joe

Think critically. When approaching the issue of the death penalty, that's the most important thing that you can do. The people on death row are human beings, not merely issues. Don't be swayed by emotions. Look at the facts and the evidence.

IV
Freedom from Bondage

No one shall be held in slavery or servitude; slavery and the slave trade shall be prohibited in all their forms.

Universal Declaration
of Human Rights
Article 4

CHAPTER 7
Trafficking

BRIEFING—BURMA, THAILAND, NEPAL, INDIA

When Lin Lin [name changed] was thirteen years old, her mother died and her father remarried. Shortly thereafter, her father took her from their Burmese village, Chom Dtong, to Mae Sai, a town just across the border in Thailand. Because she was too young to get an identity card, her father paid 35 kyats ($.30) for a travel pass for her. In Mae Sai they went to a job placement agency, where her father was given 12,000 baht ($480) from the agent, who assured him he could find a job for Lin Lin in Thailand. (That payment later became the basis of Lin Lin's bondage to her owner.)

Lin Lin and another young woman were put on a bus to Bangkok. Upon their arrival, an agent met them at a hotel and took them to Kanchanaburi, a town west of Bangkok. Lin Lin and the other girls were taken to the Ran Dee Prom brothel.

There were more than one hundred girls in brothels in Kanchanaburi. More than half of them were from Burma, and about twenty were under sixteen years old. On the third day, Lin Lin was put to work.

Lin Lin did not know what kind of work she was supposed to do until a man started touching her breasts and body. He took her to a room, told her to take off her clothes, and then forced her to have sex.

For the next two years, Lin Lin worked in four different brothels in various parts of Thailand. All but one were owned by the same family. Lin Lin thought perhaps her father knew what kind of work was in store for her, but she herself had been completely unaware.

The arrangement was the same in each brothel. The owner provided room and food, but every other expense was added to Lin Lin's "debt." She heard from the other girls that about 40 percent of the amount that each client paid was deducted from her debt. She never saw the accounts, nor was she ever told the amount of her debt. She was allowed to keep her tips.

In the first of the three brothels where she worked, Lin Lin sat in a windowed room with a number. Clients paid the owner 100 baht ($4) per hour for whichever number they wanted. Clients could take Lin Lin out all night for 800 baht ($32) by leaving an identity card or passport at the brothel. During the weekdays she had six or seven clients a day, but on the weekends the number rose to fourteen or fifteen a day.

Lin Lin saw police officers in every brothel in which she worked. They seemed to know the owners very well. They often took the girls to the rooms or out for the whole night.

Thirteen months after coming to Thailand, having worked in brothels in two towns, Kanchanaburi and Korat, Lin Lin agreed to a 5,000-baht ($200) loan because she wanted to return to Mae Sai and visit her family. The loan was to cover the bus ticket and an escort across the border; she never received any cash. When she arrived in Mae Sai, she did not have money to travel to her village. A couple approached her and said they would help her go home. They asked her to wait for them while they got their car. She agreed.When the couple arrived, there were four other girls in the car. Lin Lin got in. Instead of going home, the couple took her back into Thailand. On the road to Chiang Rai (a city in northern Thailand), she saw the driver give a policeman some money. In Chiang Rai, the girls were delivered to another agent, who had two more girls. All seven girls were driven to Klong Yai (along the Thai-Cambodian border), where they were turned over to a brothel.

In Klong Yai, Lin Lin worked with forty other young girls and women. About fifteen others were from Burma, and almost all of them were sixteen or seventeen years old. The owner told Lin Lin that she owed him for her transportation from Mae Sai to Klong Yai and for her living expenses. By that time she had no idea what she owed to whom. She assumed also that she needed to get at least 5,000 baht ($200) to pay for the earlier transportation home.

In Klong Yai, Lin Lin worked in a restaurant-cum-brothel where the men picked out which girl they wanted. Lin Lin saw the owner and pimps slap the girls often; she herself was slapped in the face and was warned that she had better do

132

whatever the client wanted. She had to work every day and was allowed only two days off per month, when she had her period.

Lin Lin never went to a doctor because she would have had to pay the expenses herself. A medical checkup cost 200 baht ($8), and Lin Lin was trying to save everything she earned to pay back her debt. Once, when she had pus and pain in her vagina, she went to the doctor, but she had to borrow money from the owner for the medicine. This amount was added to her debt.

In Klong Yai, the police had a special arrangement with the owner of the restaurant. They could take the girls for free. Every night many policemen showed up at the restaurant. Some were still dressed in full uniform, and all of them carried guns. They took Lin Lin many times without paying. (That made it harder to pay off her debt.) One time, when Lin Lin was out with another girl and two policemen for the night, the other girl insisted that her client use a condom. The policeman refused. He put a gun to her friend's head and forced her to have unprotected sex.

Lin Lin was never allowed to refuse a client. If she tried, the owner and pimps would tell her, "If you don't pay back your debt, you can stay here forever." She was warned that she would be beaten if she ever came out of the room before her client. She never tried to run away because she was afraid the owner would follow her and harm her family because she had not finished paying off her debt.

In November 1992, the Klong Yai brothel was ordered closed by government authorities. That did not stop business. Pimps stood outside the door of the closed brothel, and clients came *and negotiated with the pimps. The girls stayed in other houses and were collected or delivered to their clients. The clients could take Lin Lin anywhere they wanted. She was often sent out alone with her customer deep into the jungle. Eventually the brothel was reopened.*

On January 18, 1993, the Crime Suppression Division (CSD) raided the brothel once again. This time journalists watched and took pictures. The CSD arrested about twenty-seven girls, but no owners or pimps. The women were not allowed to take any of their belongings with them. Lin Lin had only the clothes she was wearing. She was brought first to the police station in Klong Yai. That same day she was transferred to another police station in Bangkok. The next day she was released to the NGO shelter, along with eleven other girls who were under the age of sixteen.

Lin Lin said she did not understand much about AIDS. Some clients refused to use condoms. Others did use condoms, but sometimes the condoms broke. Lin Lin was tested several times for AIDS but was never told the results.

(Lin Lin tested positive for HIV.)[1]

The trafficking of young girls and women for prostitution is an internationally recognized human rights abuse. And yet around the world, year after year, hundreds of thousands of women and girls are sold into sexual slavery. Jeannine Guthrie recently went to Nepal to interview returnees from brothels in India. Jeannine's area is Asia, specifically South Asia. In this chapter, Burmese and Nepali pseudonyms are used in place of real names.

134

Jeannine Guthrie

Researcher for Human Rights Watch/Asia

It starts with a rape. Rapes, beatings, psychological abuses. Girls forced to work in brothels are constantly told that they are worthless, that they are dirty. They are told that this is the way life is and that it happens to everybody. I've heard reports of good cop–bad cop activities inside the brothel. One person will yell at the girl and tell her that she's a whore and worthless. Another person will comfort her and say, We all go through this . . . it's a terrible thing . . . but we are a family and we care about you. This process, over a period of time, breaks down her resistance to the extent that the young woman actively begins to seek out customers.

Burmese women are trafficked to brothels in Thailand; Thai women are trafficked to Japan; Thai women are trafficked to New York; Nepali women are trafficked to India. This is a widespread abuse, with similar networking patterns all over the world. In fact, there are even indications of ties between many of the networks.

Most customers refuse to wear condoms and many of the women become HIV positive. That is one reason why the brothel owners are constantly looking for younger and younger women, for virgins. [Virgins are particularly sought after because they bring a higher price and pose less of a threat of exposure to sexually transmitted disease.][2] The statistics aren't very reliable but I have heard estimates that 40 to 60 percent of the prostitutes in Bombay are HIV-positive.

The Nepali girls I interviewed told me similar stories about their experiences. A relative offers to take a young "hill" girl to the city, usually Kathmandu, to find work in carpet factories. Sometimes the girl actually works in the factory. Other times she is not taken to Kathmandu at all, but to the Indian border, where she is handed over to a middleman who then "sells" her to a brothel.

> *When they brought me here, it was in a taxi. I kept looking around, wondering what kind of work was going on in this big city. Everywhere I looked, I saw curtained doorways and rooms in this area. Men would go and come through these curtained entrances. People on the street would be calling out, "Two rupees, two rupees." I asked the other Nepali women if these were offices; it seemed the logical explanation. In two days I knew everything. I cried.*
>
> "Tara"[3]

Trying to identify trafficking victims in Nepal is not very scientific. I had to find people who were willing to talk. To a great extent, I relied on local activists (Nepali NGOs) in each of the districts that I visited. Through these NGOs, I met women who were living in shelters and women who were back in their home villages. One local monitor, who had done a great deal of work on trafficking, came with me and interpreted.

I must say that of everything I've ever researched for Human Rights Watch, this was the hardest issue. The interviews were very painful for the victims. I worried about the psychological effect they might have on the returnees who relived their

Jeannine

humiliations once again as they told me their stories. There were times when I wondered whether it was worth it. By reporting this, could we ever make a difference? Trafficking has become an industry. A huge industry.

Most of the Nepali women who are trafficked come from ethnic groups, such as the Tamangs, a Mongolian-Tibetan tribe. There is a market in India for their particular physical type: light skin, high cheek bones, tilted eyes. The brokers get more money for them. Interestingly, those networks are composed of people from the same area. For example, if a young Tamang girl from Nuwakot is trafficked through the carpet industry to Bombay, chances are her traffickers and the brothel owners are Tamangs who come from the same district, Nuwakot.

DEBT BONDAGE

Not every woman who ends up in a brothel has been physically forced to work there. But many, many of them have been subject to some sort of coercion. Young women are cajoled, forced, and tricked into a lifestyle that they probably never expected to have. Very young girls often do not know what it means to be a prostitute. Once they arrive, they cannot leave. Most girls are not allowed out alone, ever. Their earnings are withheld.

At a certain point the girls learn to behave as everybody else in the brothel behaves. They actually encourage the customers because they need to earn a certain amount of money. If they do not earn money, they will be beaten. The women are responsible for paying back their purchase price. Every day is a scramble to make enough money, and very often the only money they actually get to keep are tips from the customers.

The women are completely dependent on the brothel owner for any kind of support. Most owners feed the girls only once or twice a day. Extra meals, clothes, and medicine come from the tips. If they aren't earning enough money, they are much more likely to be beaten. They become completely intent on their own survival: How do I get through this?

> *. . . There are several grades of prostitutes, based on beauty, hard work, "talent." The top are call girls. Then comes "bungalow," which is a higher grade of regular brothel, then comes "pillow house," which is the lowest. Most girls start out in a pillow house and work up if they do well. . . . Some girls receive training: how to approach customers, languages. During training, girls are beaten and locked in a room like a jail, but a very small one, until they stop fighting. At first a girl gets two or three clients a day, then it escalates. . . . In a pillow house, girls can have as many as forty customers a day. But they earn no money until they have paid off their debt. After they have paid off their debt, one part of their earnings goes to the gharwali [madams], one part to "local taxes," and one part to herself.*
>
> *It is one or two years before a girl is allowed out of the brothel and then, only after they have confidence she won't try to escape, she is allowed to go to the cinema or shopping with a guard from the brothel. . . . If a girl manages to escape, she is illiterate, she knows nothing about the city. She will fall victim to local people or the police.[4]*

Most of the people I talked to had either been ejected from their brothels because of an illness or managed to escape. None of them had paid off their debt. A few women do manage to pay off their debt, after years and years and years.

Often these women become recruiters and then madams themselves. Older women who have been in the industry a long time sometimes get their freedom by agreeing to find somebody to take their place. They go back to their home areas, to their villages or neighboring villages, and get a young girl to come back to India with them. The price of the new recruit essentially pays off the end of the debt.

By that point, many of the newly freed women do not have any other way of supporting themselves. They have been part of the industry for upwards of ten to fifteen years. They go independent and open their own brothels. This is an industry that perpetuates itself.

The most painful thing about the women I talked to was that because they gave in, they saw themselves as in complicity. Because of the stigma of prostitution, they felt ashamed for having given in. What else could they have possibly done? If they hadn't given in, they would be dead. On the one hand, they understood that, but at the same time, they continued to hold themselves responsible. "I was stupid . . . I was naive . . . I was young . . . I shouldn't have done such a stupid thing." Their entire self-image had gone through an awful assault.

KIDNAPPING

I spoke to one woman, in her early twenties, who had been abandoned by her husband. He went to work in India and she hadn't seen him for years. She was desperately poor and had a four-year-old child to care for. For a while she was dependent on her in-laws. Then she moved back with her parents. A neighbor told her that a man who was currently working in India wanted to marry her. Then the neighbor drugged her and kidnapped her to India. She stayed there for about ten years. I don't know her HIV status. An even sadder part was that the neighbor kidnapped this woman along with her child. When they arrived at the brothel, the neighbor told her that he was going to take the kid out and show him around the city. They never returned.

HOME, MARRIAGE, NORMAL LIVES

The goal is to go home, have a normal life, and be a respected person for having gone to India. (In the hills of Nepal, India still has an aura of respectability.) The only way that they can gain respect is to make money in Bombay. Some members of the family profit from having their daughters in Bombay. Delegations of families will send a highly placed person within the community to Bombay to collect money from the daughters who are working there. In fact, a few people *do* come back rich—a very few.

More often than not, it is a family member who actually arranges the sale—an uncle or a cousin. A few of the women pressed legal cases against their relatives, but nothing happened in any of them.

There are also local people whose job it is to keep an eye out for young girls in their district. When they see that a family situation is falling apart, there is not enough money, or a child is particularly pretty or trusting, they target the young girl as a potential trafficking victim.

Although there are very powerful anti-trafficking laws in both Nepal and India, there's a strong link between the local police and the brothels. What happens is that the police arrest the prostitute, not the brothel owners, traffickers, or pimps. Every single woman that I talked to knew something about the system of bribes that were paid to the police on a regular basis. Some reported having police as customers. There were occasional reports of political involvements. There were reports of underworld figures who provided protection. It's quite a network.

Exploiting the Exploited

It is very important to expose this industry. At the same time, here we were, asking returnees to relive their utterly horrible humiliations. We're not a relief agency. We're not going to give them anything. There may be a level of appreciation for the human contact, but that is very minor.

I did not get the sense that the returnees underwent a great catharsis by telling me their experiences. There was not the feeling on the part of those interviewed that this report would somehow contribute to the greater good. This was not like interviewing people about political issues where they see themselves as victims in a larger context. There are some women who see it that way, but they are few and far between. When something as traumatic as forced prostitution occurs, there's not a great impulse to worry about what is happening to others who are in the same position. They don't have the *luxury* of worrying about other people in a similar situation.

There has been a great deal of press coverage of trafficking in Nepal. Frequently the women are shuttled from police station to police station until they reach their home villages. Then their parents or guardians come to pick them up. While the returning women are still in police custody, somebody tips off the journalists who go to the detention center to get a personal account of trafficking. They do an interview and take pictures, which are then published in the newspaper along with the returnee's name, address, and HIV status. At that point the girl is completely compromised. It's very hard on the women involved. And on their families because their families saw the newspaper articles. They end up in NGO shelters or they go back to India, back to the streets.

I think that any report on trafficking has to be done extremely carefully. There are always times, even when I am being very careful, that I feel that I've overstepped the line. If the person I'm talking to becomes upset or angry, I think, "Oh, my God, I've done it. I've pushed it too far." There is a tendency to push hard because I need to know what happened. I need the details. I need proof.

Once this information is published, we try to follow up. We keep in touch with local organizations working on the issue. What do they need? We want to know what happens as a result of the pressure this report brings to bear on this industry. Have things gotten better or worse?

About Jeannine

I can't explain why I chose to work in this profession. Perhaps it's because I feel a sense of responsibility. My parents raised me in a Quaker meeting and the meeting placed great importance on social responsibility. Activism was an important part of my growing up.

I became involved in Asian studies at college. I visited India as an undergraduate and then went back as a graduate student. My graduate degree is in theater and drama. I wrote my master's thesis on a small social action street theater troop in Madurai, South India. The company put on plays about issues ranging from landlord-tenant disputes to political corruption, to dowry disputes, to deforestation. I'm not sure it was a great academic paper, but it was really fun to do.

I moved to New York in 1988. I was looking for something to do while I was writing my thesis. I applied to Human Rights Watch thinking it would be for a year. I was willing to do anything: copying, clipping, whatever needed to be done. It actually snowballed into a real job. I became the assistant to Sidney Jones, the executive director of Asia Watch. In 1990, Sidney asked me to take on research in Sri Lanka. From that time on I've been doing research.

As of January 1995, I became the NGO Liaison for Asia. That means I try to keep abreast of developments with all our NGO contacts in Asia. There is an essential link between the staff at Human Rights Watch and the local NGOs in their respective countries. There is no way we could sit here in New York or in Washington and monitor what's going on around the world. We have to maintain contact with people in the field.

When I returned from Nepal I was massively depressed. (I was massively depressed every day after I did an interview.) I don't necessarily get that way with other issues that I've worked on. I've done a lot of other sorts of very painful interviewing. For example, I've interviewed many refugees. Many of them have been through hell. They've seen family members killed, and watched their homes being sacked and destroyed. They've lived through a whole gamut of horrible stuff. But there is something very personal about the kind of abuse inflicted in a forced prostitution situation.

It is different because part of the abuse includes the utter destruction of personal will. It's taking somebody's personal identity and crushing it. It was hard to ask those women to describe it to me.

I have a friend in Sri Lanka who does great human rights work. She says, "The most important thing to have when you are doing this kind of work is a sense of humor." Whenever I am on assignment I try to practice the advice from my friend from Sri Lanka. But this was different.

A Message from Jeannine

Human rights work is incremental. You make a little dent here and a little dent there. You may not make a whole lot of difference, but if you think you can make a dent, you have to try. This is an uphill battle.

V
The Rights of the Child

Recalling that, in the Universal Declaration of Human Rights, the United Nations has proclaimed that childhood is entitled to special care and assistance. . . .

States Parties shall ensure that a child shall not be separated from his or her parents against their will, except when competent authorities subject to judicial review determine, in accordance with applicable law and procedures, that such separation is necessary for the best interest of the child.

The Convention on the Rights
of the Child Preamble
and Article 9

CHAPTER 8
Children of War

BRIEFING—CAMBODIA

Cambodia lies between Thailand, the Gulf of Thailand, Laos, and Vietnam. In 1941, with the help of France, Norodom Sihanouk became king of Cambodia. Fourteen years later, he abdicated the throne in favor of his father. But the new prince did not give up power. He stayed on as the premier and the leader of the main political party until 1960, when he was elected head of state.

Prince Sihanouk tried to downplay the chances of involvement in the conflict that engulfed his neighbor, Vietnam. He refused to join the Southeast Asia Treaty Organization (SEATO) and he broke off relations with both the South Vietnamese and the United States. Instead, he accepted military aid from China and allowed the North Vietnamese the use of his seaport. These declarations did not sit well with the Americans.

In 1970, with the support of the United States, General Lon Nol overthrew the government of Prince Norodom Sihanouk. All too soon, this new government became increasingly corrupt and authoritarian. Meanwhile, a secret organization sprang up in the countryside: the Khmer Rouge. This Maoist-Communist group under the leadership of Saloth Sar (known as Pol Pot) began an armed struggle to overthrow the government.

In April 1975, Pol Pot and the Khmer Rouge captured Phnom Penh, the country's capital. They drove the entire urban population out of the cities and into the countryside. At least one million people died of exhaustion and malnutrition, or from execution.

In 1979, the Vietnamese army, along with Khmer Rouge defectors headed by Heng Samrin, drove out the Khmer Rouge and established a Vietnamese-style people's republic. Pol Pot's forces were pushed to the west, near Thailand. The United Nations eventually organized camps in Thailand for the waves of Cambodians seeking food, a safe haven, or resettlement.

Chanrithy Ouk grew up in Cambodia while these events were taking place. He is currently a student at Hunter College in New York City and a volunteer with the group called Children of War. In 1990, he was invited to speak at the United Nations' celebration of the Year of the Child.

Chanrithy Ouk

Activist—Cambodia

I was born in 1970, in the second-largest city of Cambodia in the province of Battambang. It really isn't a big place, but for Cambodia, it is considered a city. I'm a New Yorker now. New Yorkers wouldn't consider my birthplace a city at all.

My father was in the police force. My mother and I lived with him in the family barracks. A few months after I was born, there was a civil war between the Khmer Rouge and Lon Nol's government.

My father was forced into the army. We were shifted from military base to military base. There were lots of kids there. We didn't have furniture or anything like that, it all belonged to the military.

In 1975, my father's side [Lon Nol's side] lost the war and the Khmer Rouge took over the country. Although I was only five, I can remember running around and crying. People were racing in all different directions. There was a lot of pushing. We ran from village to village, from place to place. I saw people being shot and bombs falling all around us. It was terrible. I was with my mom at that point and my father was with his unit somewhere.

My father took off his uniform before the Pol Pot fighters came into town. He moved away from the area where people knew him and changed his identity. When the soldiers interviewed him, he lied about everything and they didn't kill him. He said that all his papers were burned during the Vietnam

Chanrithy

War. Because the U.S. had bombed Cambodia during the Vietnam War, it was easy to make up stories about the loss of official papers.

One of the principal ideas of the Pol Pot regime was to take us out of our cities, out of our homes, and put us into a totally different place. In that way they could control us easily. We were not allowed to bring anything with us except a little food and maybe some clothing. They forced people into the forest, into mountains, and into the rice fields.

Eventually, my father found us and we moved to a hut at the edge of the mountains. I remember two things: seeing mountains and searching for things to eat. There were about a thousand of us in this place.

Soon after that, the new government decided to separate families. They grouped us together according to age. Children from five years old to fifteen were put in one camp. The others were put in different camps.

I was taken away from my parents and put in a children's camp. I still can recall it. I still remember crying for my mom. I couldn't get to her. I couldn't get to my father. I was surrounded by other children. We were all crying and looking for our parents.

My parents were put to work in different places so the three of us were completely separated. My mother was pregnant and, in the beginning, very healthy. I later found out that the authorities wouldn't give her vitamins or enough food and she grew weaker and weaker.

Khmer Rouge Children's Camp

We children were taken to the middle of nowhere. There were group leaders, several adults, who took care of all of us. Boys and girls ate together and worked together, but we slept in different areas. No one ever nurtured us. The leaders gave us little food: a little bit of rice, and soup in a big pot. The soup was mostly water, some kind of plant, and maybe one or two fishes for the whole pot. There wasn't enough protein. It affected us. We became skinny and stayed short. We had to work all the time, so none of us had time to gather our own food. Some people did all the cooking.

Each day the leaders made us do things like cut the weeds or pull up the grass or collect dead trees. Sometimes they would take us to the house of the high official and tell us to do whatever needed to be done. Garden, clean the house, or pull weeds from his fields. We had no time to be kind to other people. No one was kind to anyone. No friends. Just someone who was another copy of you.

Everything had to be shared, we couldn't own anything. There wasn't a nice bed to sleep on, that's for sure. Some of us just slept on the ground. They gave each of us a little blanket. They didn't care about building a nice shelter or anything like that. They just put something on the top of sticks, like a roof, and we stayed underneath, on the ground. There were a lot of bugs and mosquitoes. That really bothered me. Lots of children died because of the many diseases that broke out.

After a year or two, I became really sick. I was so sick and so skinny that I couldn't function as a human being anymore. I just lay on the ground by myself. No one took care of me, there was no medicine, no nothing. Somehow I managed to survive, I have no idea how.

The group leaders beat everybody. They beat us if we were too tired to work, if we talked back, for no reason at all. When they picked up a stick to beat us, we knew that there was nothing we could do.

Every night we went to bed hungry. There was never enough food. We worked around the clock and still didn't get enough food. The officials got enough food, though, because they grew fat while the rest of the people were so skinny.

The one thing that stays in my memory was the leader telling us that we were all in this together and we were one big family. He said that the whole country was like one family, and that was all we needed to focus on. They wanted to impose that ideology on everyone.

I accepted whatever they said because I thought to myself, This is the world. I didn't know that there were other countries. I didn't even know that the earth was round. I'd look up and see the sky so high and think to myself, Is this just space or is it something somewhere? All pictures and books were banned, so none of us knew anything about the outside world.

I did get an education at the camp. Lesson one: Kids who tried to escape were killed. There was no way to escape. Lesson two: The Khmer Rouge were not good people. Lesson three: Either stay with the Khmer Rouge or kill yourself.

Meanwhile, my father was forced to work in a rice field. He had a hard time of it because he had never farmed in his life. But he learned fast. He had to because it was the only way he could survive. He saw my mother just a few times. Later, I learned that my mom became very sick while giving birth to a child. There was no medicine to help her. She was suffering from starvation and so she died. The child passed away two days later because nobody took care of it. I had no image of my mother until much later, when I saw a picture of her. When I saw the picture, I saw the lady who gave birth to me and that's it. For me it is not normal to call someone "Mother." Basically, I consider myself my own parent because my mother passed away and my father wasn't with me. After my mother died, my father was encouraged to marry another lady, who is now my stepmother.

When I turned eight, I began to realize that this was not the right way to live. I didn't know where my parents were. I was hungry all the time. I was forced to work.

Then, my father got permission from the Khmer Rouge to visit me for a few hours every once in a while. When he came to see me, he had to explain that he was my father. I knew that he must be right because he always looked for me and not for the other children.

THE VIETNAMESE INVADE CAMBODIA

When the Vietnamese invaded Cambodia, they installed a new government and opened the schools. The country was really messed up by then. People began searching the countryside for their relatives. My father came to get me. He was so happy that the war was over and the Khmer Rouge were gone. He didn't actually say anything, he just grabbed me and carried me away. We were two crazy people trying to survive, trying to get away from the mess. Even though we didn't talk about it, I had the feeling that I was going to be better off.

I was very happy that we were together, and we vowed never to be separated again. I felt a sense of freedom for the first time. We couldn't settle anywhere permanently because there was still fighting, even though the Vietnamese were declared the winner.

During that period, my stepmother gave birth to a child, my half sister. My stepmother and I didn't really get along that well. She had her own child and I was from my father's old wife. She probably felt jealous that my father treated me so well. Once the baby was born, she made me take care of her. Whenever I refused to do it, she'd beat me. When my father was away, she cursed me. As soon as he came home, I'd tell on her and she would become nice. Once my father went away again, she'd continue beating me.

Eventually, my father took me to his mother's house. I had never met my grandmother. She lived in a wood farmhouse in a small village located next to a river. Somehow I had the terrible idea that he would leave me there. I stayed close to him all the time. At night I tried to keep myself awake. He knew that I knew that he was going to leave me. Once I couldn't help but fall asleep. In the morning when I awoke, he was gone.

I woke up and began crying because I immediately knew that he had left me. My grandmother and the other relatives who lived in the house tried to comfort me. I cried for days and couldn't settle down. It was a terrible time.

My aunts and uncles were nice enough, but they were strangers. When they introduced themselves and told me how we were related, I really didn't care all that much. A few days later, after I stopped crying, I went to plant crops in the rice fields with my uncle. He gave me food and life got a little bit better.

Phnom Penh

In 1981, I moved to Phnom Penh with my uncle and his family. It was the first time I saw Cambodia's capital. I saw buildings. That was an exciting thing. Pol Pot never took care of the city. There was a lot of dirt and buildings were falling apart. But it was so different for me. It was not just a piece of land. There was cement. I had never seen cement.

When my uncle told me that I was going to go to school, I didn't know what that was. The first day I was so quiet. I just went in, sat down, and looked around. I didn't see anyone I knew. It was exciting to have new people around me. Nevertheless, I didn't want to stay there. On the second day I ran out of the classroom. The teacher brought me back, but he didn't beat me. He talked to me in a very nice way. So I sat down quietly and tried to figure out what school was. I asked myself, "What do I want from school? Is it my job to come to school?"

After a few days I got used to it and went every day. I learned how to write the Cambodian alphabet, which is completely different from English or Chinese. It's related to Thai, a very graphic form of writing. That was the first time I learned about language. I also learned to add and subtract numbers. The teachers taught me to count with my fingers. I was amazed when the numbers I counted on the fingers of my hands came out the same as the symbols on the page. Remarkable: counting, numbers, language. This was a whole new world. I was almost ten years old.

I met many Vietnamese people in Phnom Penh and realized that there was another country beside Cambodia. I also began to learn about a thing called "religion." The older relatives went to a [Buddhist] temple and sometimes I went with them.

I liked going there because I got food for free. That's what I cared about most, food. People actually brought food to the temple. They prayed to their dead ancestors and asked them for blessings of happiness and peace. I liked that idea. As I got older, I began to understand better the ideas behind giving food to the temple.

In 1985 I experienced another big change. I hadn't heard anything about my father in years. I assumed that he was dead. Cambodia was a Communist country and it was very hard to have a connection with an outside country. My father could not write because it would be unsafe for us if the Vietnamese knew that we had a relative outside the country. I learned that there was a possibility that my father was alive and living in a place called a "refugee camp." I learned about these camps through government programs on radio and TV. I started thinking about my father. I thought maybe I could escape to these camps and look for him.

When I finished fourth grade, I was fifteen years old and getting close to the age when the Vietnamese drafted kids like me into the army. They would either relocate me to Vietnam or to the jungle to confront the remaining Khmer Rouge. It was no longer safe to stay in the city. My cousin, who was about my age, and I decided to leave Cambodia. His parents gave us some money to use for bribes.

It took us a few days to get to the province next to the Thai border. We had to walk because there were no roads between Cambodia and Thailand. It was very complicated on the border because the whole area was a war zone, a mined war zone. Vietnam and Thailand were enemies. In between these two enemies was what was left of the Khmer Rouge forces.

There were some people who guided Cambodians across

the border. These guides knew where the mines were and they charged a lot of money to those who wanted to cross. They worked for gold or silver only.

One night a group of people hired a guide to help them escape. My cousin and I didn't have enough money. We gave the guide everything that we had and he allowed us to follow behind the group. During the day we hid in a jungle so thick you couldn't see anyone through it. We slept until five or six o'clock in the evening, when it started to get dark. We never knew who we would be confronting: Vietnamese troops, the Khmer Rouge, or another group just out to rob or kill us. It took us a whole week to get across the border, which was about ten to twenty miles away. There were places where we had to go a long way around because of the minefields. Every once in a while we heard about people stepping on a mine and getting blown up. I was frightened. I thought if my life ended here there was nothing I could do, but if I got lucky, I would find my father. Everyone in my group arrived safely.

REFUGEE CAMP IN THAILAND

When we finally made it to the camps I became so excited. This was the first time I came in contact with organizations specially designed to help, not hurt, people. For example, there was the United Nations High Commissioner for Refugees, the Red Cross, and many other international organizations. We were given shelter, food, blankets, and clothes. I got my very own shoes. I got free food all the time. I thought to myself, I can live with this. I could stay here for the rest of my life.

As soon as we arrived, I went to the office of the Red Cross and met other people who were trying to find their relatives in the camps. There were flyers with lists of people. I searched the list looking for my father's name. All I knew was his first name. I didn't know his last name. I didn't know his birthday. I didn't even know my own birthday.

My father used to call me by the nickname "Pros." When I met his family they gave me another nickname: "March." So I had two names when I didn't know my real name. That wasn't much to give to the Red Cross. Eventually, my cousin's parents wrote us a letter and told us my father's last name. It wasn't an official letter, as we were afraid to send anything officially. It was delivered by hand by a new refugee.

Once I knew my father's name, I gave it to the Red Cross. He wasn't in any of their camps. They began checking the names of all the people who left the camps to go to countries that took in Cambodian refugees. The list was huge.

Then a new problem arose. When my cousin and I arrived at the camp, a married couple invited us to live with them and share their food. At first, the man was very nice. Little did I know that they were the types who looked for people who had relatives in a third country, like the U.S. or Canada, and extorted money from them. The United Nations personnel didn't know about this and no one would tell them. The man told people that he was my caretaker, but he really wasn't. I was old enough to take care of myself. Besides, all our supplies came from the U.N. I began to realize that I should not depend on other people, or even the U.N., to do things for me. I needed to do things for myself.

The man, my "caretaker," turned out to be one of the cruelest people in the camp. I suspect that he was once part of the

Pol Pot regime because he behaved unlike an ordinary citizen. He had no feelings, he abused his wife, and he drank every day.

One day, a European man came looking for me. He spoke English but I don't know his nationality. He said, "We found your father."

"My father?"

"Yes."

I was speechless. He told me that my father was living in New York. I didn't know about New York. I had heard about America. I heard that it was the best place in the world. The people in the camps applied to America as the first choice. America was a big deal for refugees in the camp.

I began studying English. I attended the free school sessions set up by the U.N. and listened outside the window of the pay school when they taught English.

Once my cruel caretakers found out that my father was in America, they demanded that he send them three thousand U.S. dollars, a lot of money when you change it into Thai currency. My father wrote and said that he didn't see any reason to give them money. The man threatened to kill me. He said that nobody would know if I was dead or alive because the international organizations couldn't investigate every missing-persons case.

I went to the office of the International Red Cross and told them about my situation. Then the case blew up. They moved me to another place, but the man threatened my cousin.

The International Red Cross immediately told my father and he did everything he could to get me out of the camp. My father sent me a little money so that I could get additional food for myself and my cousin. The man took all of it. Eventually, my father sent the man five hundred dollars just to make things easier for me. He implied that if the man left me alone, he would send a little more money.

My father became the sponsor for both my cousin and me. He sent us documentation and papers. The authorities needed to know for sure that I was really my father's son. I had to memorize my birth date, the names of my half brother and half sister, my stepmother's name, and my father's last name. Here I was, a person with no sense of family, now faced with a huge family, names, dates, and so on. I studied those documents like crazy.

One night my cousin tried to escape because he was convinced that the American embassy wouldn't take both of us. (At that point they took only those who were directly related to the sponsor. Later, my father provided my cousin with enough money to get an identification card that enabled him to become a citizen of Thailand. He's now a Thai citizen, married to a Thai girl.)

From the border camp I was taken to another camp deeper in Thailand. I stayed there for medical treatment for six months. Then they flew me to New York.

I was so excited at the thought of going somewhere in a plane. When I got in the airplane I worried what would happen if I needed to go to the bathroom. But the airport workers gave us a little orientation. I didn't know that they would give me food on the plane. European food. It turned out to be some kind of chicken dish. I didn't like it, and I didn't want to finish it in case I had to use the bathroom. I was worried about the plane dumping the waste on people's heads.

New York City

My plane landed at Kennedy Airport and I cried like a baby. Here I was, eighteen years old and crying like I was five. It was very embarrassing. I didn't recognize my father at first because he was wearing a suit and a tie. He looked completely different. I hadn't seen him for nine years.

My father was crying, too. That's when I knew that he loved me. That's when I knew I had a family after all. It's just that we didn't do it the normal way. We did it in a very indirect way. Until now.

The first thing my father did was take my small luggage from my hand and put it in the trunk of his car. The second thing he did was tell me my real name, Chanrithy. I think it's a very nice name. "Chan" means Monday and "rith" means spiritual power.

The big city with all its lights and buildings was amazing. I thought to myself, "I'm safe. I won't have to go through those difficulties again. I can live happy here."

A Message from Chanrithy

By listening to other people and sharing their experiences, you will learn to care for others and respect their existence deeply.

Chanrithy, aged three or four, with his father.

If the Khmer Rouge had found this picture, Chanrithy's father would have been killed, so he wrapped it in plastic and buried it in the woods. Later, he dug it out and brought it with him to the United States.

CHAPTER 9

No Child Should Be Caged

BRIEFING—JAMAICA

The International Covenant on Civil and Political Rights and the United Nations Rules for the Administration of Juvenile Justice require that children suspected of offenses be separated from adults if detained. The Juveniles Act of Jamaica contains similar protection for children charged with a crime.

In June 1994, Human Rights Watch/Children's Rights Project sent a monitor to investigate lockups and juvenile correctional institutions in the Kingston–St. Andrew area of Jamaica. She interviewed more than forty children who were in detention. She also spoke with the commissioner of correctional services, the commissioner of police and many other senior police and juvenile correctional officials. Everyone was very cooperative.

Michelle India Baird

Counsel for Human Rights Watch/Children's Rights Project

I was surprised at Jamaica's openness. The officials said that I could go anywhere, visit any institution. In fact, they arranged for my visits. They knew that the kids were there, and knew that the situation in the lockups where people were held awaiting trials was especially bad. Right before I arrived, one lockup had been closed because three men had suffocated in the cell. This event made world headlines.

Governments usually know when a human rights monitor is in their country. Some countries have flat out refused us entry to their prisons. Other countries worry about their international reputation and let us in. Jamaica, which receives international funding from the World Bank and revenues from tourism, wants to maintain a good image.

The first person I met was the commissioner of police. He said, "Well, yes, you will find children in the lockup. There's nothing we can do. There is only one lockup that holds forty-eight boys, and that was already overcrowded." (There are no centers for girls. Girls are held in foster homes.) The children's facilities are away from city centers and it's a hassle for the police to drive out there.

The one police officer designated as the juvenile officer had never visited the lockups, even though she was within walking distance of one of them. She told me that she had not been given a police car so she "couldn't go there." It was an easy walk.

Michelle

The officer was friendly. She felt, as most people do when they can't perform a job properly, very frustrated. She sat in a windowless office that had no files. She had just gotten a phone. She was the stepchild of the police department. Having another person, me, take her seriously, brought her out.

LOCKUPS

As we approached the first lockup, I smelled the worst odor imaginable. I had visited many police stations when I lived in South Africa. Even though there was a lot of abuse, the prisons there were usually clean. This was a big surprise to me.

A sign on the wall stated that seven children were being held. They had them in one cell, separated from the adults. However, adult prisoners roamed around the facilities and many of them hung around the kids' cell. I couldn't tell who was an officer and who was a prisoner because no one wore uniforms. As we walked down the hall a rat ran across our path.

The two-story building held about twenty cells. The downstairs was almost completely dark because the lights didn't work. There was no light coming from the outside because most of the men stuffed paper in the small windows to keep the insects out. There were cells on both sides of the hallways with the toilets at the ends. All of the toilets were overflowing. It looked as though they hadn't worked in ages. There was a gully that ran down both sides of the cells. Men were urinating into the hallway. They threw the waste buckets in the hall as well. The kids were jailed at the end of the floor. Because the building was on a slant, waste was running into their cell.

The policewoman was appalled. "How can they expect us to work in these conditions?" That surprised me.

One of the kids' parents brought a big piece of cardboard for the kids to block the flow of waste. It didn't work very well. While I was there the authorities gave the kids water to sweep out the floors.

When I began interviewing the kids, they told me that usually their requests for water were denied. Some of the boys had been pushed around and beaten when they were arrested, but not while they were in the cells.

What was most surprising was the sense of camaraderie among the kids. They took care of each other. When I talked to one, he would say, "Make sure you talk to so-and-so, too, because such-and-such happened to him."

These kids were not street children, but all of them were poor. One fifteen-year-old, who was so small he looked twelve, was arrested because he got into a fight with another boy over a girl they both liked. The police broke up the fight and arrested him, not the other boy.

> *A policeman put a gun to my head and asked me what I was doing. I didn't say anything. The policeman said, "If you don't tell us we're going to kill you."*
>
> *"I didn't do anything," I told him. And he pulled the trigger, but the gun wasn't loaded. I almost died, I was so scared. My neighbors started yelling, "Leave him alone! Leave that boy alone!" And they stopped and took me to jail.*

There were seven kids in the cell, which was about eight by ten. Besides the raw sewage seeping onto the concrete floor, there were no beds, no sheets, no blankets, and no mattresses. The kids slept on the concrete floor. They put down pieces of cardboard or their own shirts to protect themselves from the filth as best they could. It didn't work very well. Sometimes the guards gave them water to wash down the sewage.

Most of the kids had stuck their shoes in the bars to keep them away from the sewage. I had to throw away the shoes that I was wearing because they were caked with the stuff. I was literally walking through shit.

The second lockup was in an old concrete building. Each cell was made up of thick walls, solid steel doors that had dime-size air holes in them, and a high two-inch window that gave out a little light but provided no ventilation. There were eight boys in one cell that was on the top floor. One of the boys said, "It's like hell in here. Our cell is like hell. See what it is like, ask them to let you close the door."

There were insects crawling all over the walls and all over the boys. The boys had been denied medical attention and they had a fungus-like rash. The authorities explained that although the doctor came once a month, he had been sick recently, so had not been there.

The policewoman was repulsed and wanted to leave. I insisted that I interview each of them individually, privately. I went into the cell. When the boys were taken into the hall to wait their turn to be interviewed, they were thrilled because there was a breeze running down the hallway. They said, "Oh, a breeze. Thank you. Thank you. We haven't had a breeze."

One of the boys had asthma and the guard wouldn't give him his pump. The boy said, "I need my pump." Another boy piped up, "Yeah, the other night we thought he was going to die. He started choking and coughing and we thought he was going to die. We yelled for water. Nobody brought us water. We started collecting water out of a milk carton that we set up outside the window." (There was a drip that comes down off the building.) The policewoman was quite moved by this young boy.

Nobody ever listens to these children. They are so ready to share information. None of the kids said that he had a lawyer. I had to be very careful not to raise their expectations. I said that I was not their lawyer and I couldn't represent them, but I would speak to people who are responsible.

These conditions have not stopped crime in Jamaica. In fact, I was told that more children are being arrested because they are becoming more violent. But most of the boys I talked to had not committed serious crimes; it was usually petty theft, fistfights. One boy threw a rock through a neighbor's window.

One boy really got to me. I was interviewing judges and observing family court. At one point I went down to the holding cells because that's where I could meet a lot of them who would be more willing to talk because the guards weren't there. I did this when I worked in South Africa.

I met a sixteen-year-old who had been kept in the cell with the sewage for forty-two days. He told me that a neighbor had accused him of stealing a motorcycle. He said that he didn't do it. The motorcycle had since been returned, but he was still in jail. This was his first offense. In this case the boy's mother and aunt got money to pay for a lawyer to appear in court. His mother brought her son clean clothes to wear in court. She was so worried. There was so much concern there. His aunt said, "We know why this happened. This man had been sexually interested in the mother. When she refused his advances, he wanted to get even."

The boy wanted to go back to school. He worried that he was going to be behind in his studies. He was a good kid. The lawyer came and spoke to him for two minutes. The lawyer looked at me and demanded, "Who are you?" I told him who I was with and he became more pleasant. I didn't know how much he knew about the case so I said, "Do you know he awaited trial for forty-two days in the police lockup?"

"What!" he yelled. "A kid's not supposed to be held at police stations. He should be moved to the juvenile facilities." I said, "I know." I was so upset my voice quaked. He said he would talk to the judge immediately. The judge told the lawyer that he would take that into consideration when he tried the case. During the trial the accuser said, "Well, I don't know if this is the boy. But somebody did it and somebody's going to pay." The judge decided to release the boy on bail. The mother was ecstatic about that and the kid was, too. I was shocked. It seemed to me that the judge should have dropped the charges right there and let him go home.

This decision made me very upset. The mother said she had to go and get bail, which was set at a thousand Jamaican dollars (about $300 U.S.). This was much more than she could afford. Before I left, I gave both the boy and his mother my business card.

Two days later I was on a tour of a lockup. I was walking through this dark, vile place and heard somebody calling my name. "Michelle. Michelle." It was the boy. His mother didn't have enough for bail because she had borrowed so much money to pay the lawyer. The boy was standing there in tears, clutching my card, which was all crumpled up. He wore no clothes, just shorts. "What are you doing here?" I asked. When he explained I said, "This is ridiculous." I turned to the policewoman who was escorting me. "I saw this boy two days ago, he was supposed to be released on bail. He's not supposed to be here." I was furious. It seemed the lawyer had not taken responsibility for the boy, that he didn't try to raise bail even though he knew they could get bail bonds. I understand that lawyers are overworked, but it seemed he should have at least done that.

The policewoman was also shocked. She called the judge and the boy was released that afternoon. That really made me happy. The boy was thrilled.

The most difficult thing for me was leaving Jamaica. I can't forget the children's faces or their individual stories. I don't see them just as statistics for a report that goes to the U.N., supposedly to bring about change. Supposedly.

When I visit awful conditions in places like the prisons of Jamaica, you'd think I'd be revolted. I see the people, not the filth.

ABOUT MICHELLE

When I was still in high school, I thought about becoming a lawyer and representing kids who had been charged with crimes. I have no idea why. It seemed to me that children were not treated fairly. I grew up in Tennessee, near Nashville. The first time I went to a prison was during a high school class trip. We met some of the prisoners and ate lunch there. It really interested me and I wanted to learn more. The school used the trip as a scare tactic, but I became curious about what was happening to the prisoners.

In 1982 I went to the University of Mississippi, partly because I was curious about the history of the South. During my freshman year, I became friends with the guy who was the first African-American cheerleader for the University of Mississippi. The cheerleaders carried the flag across the football field before the games. The symbol of the school was a Confederate flag.

My friend was pressured by a number of groups who wished to make this issue public. They did not want him to carry the flag. The cheerleader was conflicted. On one hand, he felt that he was breaking ground just by being elected to the position of cheerleader. On the other hand, it would be ridiculous for a black person to march around a football field with a Confederate flag.

That night, one of my new friends, a five-foot-two blonde debutante from a small town in Mississippi, rushed into my room, all excited. She said that students were protesting at the student center. "Let's go." I went because when you're in college and something is happening, you go.

The NAACP and other groups were meeting with the administration about the flag. About a thousand white students, angry about the risk of losing their flag, were throwing clumps of red Mississippi mud at the building where the meeting was taking place. The students were screaming and yelling. There were two black fraternities on campus and my cheerleader friend was a member of one of them. Everybody decided to continue the protest in front of the frat house. I was so naive. I knew the issues, but I didn't understand the anger.

It was raining and there was mud everywhere because the black frats didn't have beautiful lawns as all the white ones had. People started picking up mud and throwing it at the fraternity house. I was shocked. I couldn't believe what I was seeing.

As I turned to my friend to say, "I can't believe it," she was throwing this big thing of mud at the house and yelling, *"Nigger."*

"What's going on here?" I screamed. I was shocked and confused and wanted to leave the university at once. I ended up staying, though, and learned a lot by living in Mississippi. That incident mobilized me to become an activist.

A MESSAGE FROM MICHELLE

Don't be afraid to speak up. Ask questions. Never doubt that you are important. Your words, your actions can make extraordinary differences.

VI
The Right to Vote

• (1) Everyone has the right to take part in the government of his country, directly or through freely chosen representatives.

• (2) Everyone has the right of equal access to public service in his country.

• (3) The will of the people shall be the basis of the authority of government; this will shall be expressed in periodic and genuine elections which shall be by universal and equal suffrage and shall be held by secret vote or by equivalent free voting procedures.

Universal Declaration
of Human Rights
Article 21

CHAPTER 10

A National Election

BRIEFING—TAJIKISTAN

Tajikistan is a mountainous country of 5.1 million people that borders China, Uzbekistan, Kyrgyzstan, and Afghanistan. In the early nineties, opposition to years of Communist control led to prodemocracy demonstrations in Dushanbe, Tajikistan's capital.

September 9, 1991: The country declared its independence from the Soviet Union. Rahman Nabiev, a former CPT (Communist Party of Tajikistan) leader, became acting president and a state of emergency was imposed.

After a week of civil unrest, Nabiev lifted the state of emergency and called for a democratic election. Nabiev won the election with 58 percent of the vote. To outside observers, however, the voting had been rigged.

March 1992: Tajikistan became a member of the United Nations and was given diplomatic recognition by the United States. President Nabiev enjoyed considerable support in rural areas of his country, but his rule was challenged by Islamic and pro-democracy groups. A bloody civil war began three months later and lasted for six months. During that time more than 20,000 people died and 500,000 were left homeless.

December 2: The Supreme Soviet (parliament) of Tajikistan met, with the idea of creating a new government that would include all the parties. Instead, it elected a government that was controlled by the previous Communist old guard, headed by Emomali Rahmanov. Meanwhile, Russia sent 20,000 troops as part of a "peace-keeping" force, but many observers allege that they really did it to prop up the government.

April 1994: The Rahmanov government and the opposition engaged in United Nations–sponsored peace negotiations. An agreement on cessation of hostilities was signed on September 17, 1994. In November Rahmanov was elected president with 60 percent of the vote.[1]

Ten months prior to the election, Human Rights Watch received funding to set up an office in Tajikistan. Human Rights Watch wanted a field presence there in order to monitor the abuses taking place daily. This was thought necessary because the human rights violations during and after the brutal civil war were quite extensive.

Fatemeh Ziai
Researcher for Human Rights Watch/Helsinki

In November 1994, a presidential election was held in Tajikistan. It was clear to anyone who had spent time there that this was not going to be a free election. There was a lot of fear and intimidation. The election law had serious flaws. There was no freedom of expression because the press was strictly controlled and opposition political parties were banned. Many refugees from the civil war were unable to vote because they had not yet returned home. Finally, there was very little time between the announcement of the election and the actual election date.

You can't just monitor an election on the actual day; you need to observe throughout the entire campaign period. A number of conditions have to be present, such as freedom of expression, freedom of assembly, and the ability to form political parties freely.

Then, on election day, you need to cover the polling booths as thoroughly as possible, as was done in the South African elections, not just have a token presence.

During the pre-election period the government never tried to stop me in my investigations. The officials were preoccupied with winning the election. I traveled around the country in a very dumpy Russian car. I preferred to travel that way because when I went into villages to do investigative work, I didn't want to attract attention.

Pre-election

Throughout this period there was a campaign of intimidation. People were scared. They still had vivid memories of paramilitary forces and thugs, supporters of the government, coming in and beating people up if they were on the "wrong" side. During the civil war, hundreds of thousands of people had been

Fatemeh

driven out of their homes, their farms had been destroyed, their cattle had been stolen, and their possessions looted. Very slowly they'd returned and were trying to rebuild their lives.

Even though most people were scared to talk about the intimidation, I did manage to find some who would speak out. There is always someone who is willing to talk. They told me that officials had come into their village and, with varying degrees of threat in their voices, said, "If we find out that *anybody* in this village didn't vote for Rahmanov, you'll be sorry."

The villagers were afraid that the authorities would find out if they voted for the "wrong" person. They knew that this wasn't going to be a fair election and most thought that it would be better to play it safe.

I asked people, "Do you feel that the government has a way of knowing who voted for whom?"

And they would answer, "Yes."

They were persuaded that their vote was going to be public. By this time, people in Tajikistan had gone through so much suffering that they were unwilling to take risks. Many thought, "Fine, let's just vote for Rahmanov and have some peace and quiet in the weeks following the election."

I did meet one elderly woman who insisted that she was going to vote for [Abdulmalik] Abdulajanov, the opponent of Rahmanov. I asked, "Aren't you afraid? Everybody in your village is afraid to vote for him."

"I'm going to vote for him and I don't care if they come in here and kill me. I'm going to vote for whoever I want because they can't get away with this kind of thing."

Along with the right to vote comes the right *not* to vote. The citizens of Tajikistan were afraid not to vote. Even though they had no concrete proof, people believed that if only a small number from their village voted, thugs would later come in and beat everybody up. Because of this climate of fear, the voter turnout was very high.

As the time for the election drew nearer, international organizations refused to monitor it because the environment in the country was not conducive to a democratic election. Human Rights Watch made it a point not to be present as an official monitor. We didn't want to give the government the opportunity to put pictures of a Human Rights Watch representative on television as a way of showing that their election was open and democratic. The U.S. Embassy and the United Nations also had people to observe the election "unofficially." As predicted, the Tajik government later tried to turn the presence of these observers to its advantage by saying that U.N. and U.S. monitors had been present.

A few days before the election, Human Rights Watch wrote a report and issued a press release:

FOR IMMEDIATE RELEASE

TAJIK parliamentary elections will not be free or fair.

Human Rights Watch/Helsinki is deeply concerned that the parliamentary elections scheduled for February 26 in Tajikistan may be seriously flawed. . . . The electoral law bans the participation of opposition parties, limits the number of candidates allowed to be registered, allows the under-representation of ethnic minorities and women and thus seriously jeopardizes the fairness of the elections.[2]

This press release included a series of recommendations on the reforms needed in order for the election to be truly democratic.

ELECTIONS

The day of the election, an international delegation that comprised representatives from the CIS [Commonwealth of Independent States], Turkey, Iran, India and others, trooped around and looked at whatever the government wanted them to see. Video cameras followed them everywhere. It was a photo op. They did not have an opportunity to observe the election in a meaningful manner.

On election day I visited as many polling stations as I could, about fifteen of them. I also spoke with unofficial monitors from embassies and other interested organizations. You would think that at least during the time that we were there the election officials would make an effort to cover things up, but we all observed violations.

Often an official would stop me as I entered a polling station and ask what I was doing there. I'd tell them who I was and show my identification card to prove that I worked with an organization that was accredited by the ministry of foreign affairs. I'd try to engage them with simple, chatty questions as an excuse to stay a while and watch what was going on.

There were thugs hanging around the polling stations. The voters were registered upon arrival and given a ballot with the two candidates' names on it. They simply had to put a check in front of the name of the person who they were voting for and then drop the paper into a box. It wasn't very complicated.

The literacy rate is very high in Tajikistan and most people can read. In many cases these thugs would accompany voters into the polling booth, supposedly to show them how to vote. There were also cases of ballot stuffing. (I collected testimony from other international organizations who were unofficial monitors as well.)

POST-ELECTION

The really egregious violations didn't take place in the polling stations. Government officials collected all the votes from the polling stations, and the electoral commission, which is appointed by the government, did the final count. There was no method of verification, no control. At that point they could have announced any result they chose. Everything was done in pencil, because that's the way it was always done in the former Soviet Union.

Human Rights Watch was the only organization in Tajikistan that came right out immediately after the election, and said that it had been fraudulent. The Tajik government did not react well to this. This election was important to them. They were trying to portray themselves as a democracy. Then suddenly, here comes a press release that is picked up by the foreign press and the wire services.

A high ranking official (who must remain nameless) called me into his office and said that he was very disappointed in me. He said that he felt that we always had a very close relationship, that the lies that I wrote didn't look very good for my organization, and that everybody knew that there had been no fraud.

"I reported only what happened," I replied. "Whenever I heard a report that I couldn't verify, I didn't include it in the press release. Everything that I put in was confirmed." I felt strongly that my work was accurate and I actually believe that deep down he realized that.

FATEMEH IN TAJIKISTAN

When I left for Tajikistan, I knew that I would be leaving my family and friends in America to go to a rather remote place. I remember thinking that I probably wouldn't have a social life, so I spent about $500 on books before I left New York. The amazing thing was that I didn't even have time to read.

When I first arrived, I thought, what do I do now? I didn't have to think too hard because within a week people were knocking on my door with their problems. They learned about me through friends, families, and other international organizations who couldn't do anything about human rights abuses because it wasn't within their mandate.

My one-room office-apartment was in the Hotel Tajikistan, an old tourist hotel that was probably nice once upon a time, but was now way past its glory days. In the hotel were a few U.N. offices, the International Committee of the Red Cross, and several other international organizations. But worst of all, the place was crawling with Russian soldiers who were usually drunk and always armed. Drinking and arms are a bad combination. I did not feel safe at all.

More important, I did not think that it was safe for the people who were coming to see me. The average Tajiks who visited me had to pass by a number of guards just to get into the hotel. Often they were turned away. It was impossible for me to work because this was not a discrete environment.

Eventually I moved into an apartment across the street from the hotel. It was considered a luxury apartment, but everything is relative. The building was a quaint, three-story pink building designed in an Islamic style with big arched windows. The woman who lived there was a Russian, whose husband had been a major in the Soviet army. She was from Siberia and wanted to go back to visit her family, but she couldn't afford the trip. It was a godsend. I paid her $150 a month, which is an incredible amount of money in Tajikistan, where people usually pay rent of ten dollars a month. My new apartment had a kitchen and a bathroom. The best thing about it was that it usually had hot water. All kinds of people came over just to take a bath in my apartment.

At first the government welcomed me, not because of the organization that I represented—our organization was never particularly welcomed—but as an individual. I was born in Iran. For the average Tajik, Iran is the most fascinating country in the world. The officials speak Farsi (the Iranian national language) and love Iranian culture, literature, and music—especially pop music. I really took advantage of that in the first few months.

In the capital most people speak Russian, but in the small villages they speak Tajik, which is very similar to Farsi. Most women don't speak Russian at all, so when outsiders came to interview them, the men would usually do all the talking. The women have so much to say, but if the listener only speaks Russian, there is little communication.

The interesting thing was that in most of the cases that involved human rights abuses, the men were more afraid to speak out than the women. Women were not likely to be attacked by the government in the same way as men.

During those first months, people came and told me about problems they were having with the government. For example, a woman would tell me that the Ministry of Security (previously the KGB [the secret police]) had come to her house and taken away her husband. The next day when she went to the Security offices, officials would deny that he was being held there.

I would go to the Ministry of Security and show the guard my accreditation card which says, Human Rights Watch/Helsinki. Transliterated into Russian, it reads like, "khiumanrautsvotchkhelsinki" Although the guard had no idea what that meant, he'd ring up the minister and say, "An Iranian woman wants to see the minister." My Iranian heritage was the passport that got me in the front door.

Once inside, I'd ask what the charges were against this person. If the person was someone obscure, they'd often let him go because it wasn't worth their while for an international organization to make a deal over him. When people weren't released, Human Rights Watch would often launch a formal protest.

Several months passed and I began writing reports and press releases that were picked up by the wire services and other media, including Russian TV stations. Once that happened, the government officials became very unhappy with me. Doors shut and phone calls went unanswered. I would have to stand outside an official's office for literally hours, insisting that he see me.

About Fatemeh

I was born in Shiraz, Iran, but I grew up in Tehran. My father is a pediatrician and my mother is a homemaker. My father had to become a feminist because he had four daughters, no sons. He encouraged us to pursue professions. My older sister is a doctor. The second one is an architect, I went to law school, and my little sister went to business school.

Before the Iranian revolution, my country was quite westernized in many respects. I remember my childhood as idyllic, but it was also sheltered. It was only after my family moved to the States that I realized what had been happening in Iran.

The Iranian Revolution

In 1963 the shah of Iran, Muhammad Reza Pahlavi, inaugurated an ambitious program to modernize the country. The reforms were too much for some and not enough for others and were accompanied by corruption and widespread social dislocation. As opposition grew, particularly among the clergy, order was kept by the army and the secret police, Savak.

In 1978, opposition from both the left and the right led to rioting. The shah placed Iran under military rule. Opposition continued from Paris from the exiled Islamic leader, Ayatollah Ruhollah Khomeini. On January 6, 1979, the shah lifted military rule and a few days later left the country. Khomeini returned to a joyous welcome on February 1, and on the twelfth proclaimed Iran an Islamic republic. Hundreds of the shah's supporters and alleged members of Savak were arrested, tried, and executed. Khomeini initiated policies to reverse the Westernization of Iran.3

The revolution and all the upheaval that came with it affected me very much. Even though we were no longer living in Iran, we felt that our world was falling apart. The lives of my grandmother, my uncles, my aunts, my cousins, and my friends had turned upside down. Several of my relatives were jailed and people we had known were executed because of their involvement with the shah's regime.

After high school I went to Brown University, where I became very interested in political causes. I started a Middle Eastern Students Association there. I majored in history, but out of curiosity, I took a class in Russian. Because Iran shared a border with the Soviet Union, the Russian language had always felt very close. Besides, I really like languages. The teacher was fabulous and I got very involved. I took an intensive course during my freshman year. I studied a second year and then went to Moscow to study for a summer. It turned out to be very useful because in Tajikistan I spoke as much Russian as Tajik.

Then I went on to Harvard Law School. A human rights journal started during my first year and I later became an editor on it. This experience was one of the reasons I became interested in working with Human Rights Watch several years later.

After graduation I practiced at a big New York law firm, but I was not happy. I liked the firm, the people, and the environment, but I found the work so unsatisfying. We worked really long hours and I did not have time to live my own life. I worked really long hours in Tajikistan, too, but the difference was that I loved what I was doing in Tajikistan.

A Message from Fatemeh:

If there is a cause that interests you, follow your heart. By following my heart I finally found a career that gives me incredible satisfaction. My satisfaction comes from doing something intellectually rewarding, as well as knowing that I have the opportunity to help people who might otherwise be defenseless.

VII
The Road Toward Democracy

All human beings are born free and equal in dignity and rights. They are endowed with reason and conscience and should act towards one another in a spirit of brotherhood.

Universal Declaration
of Human Rights
Article 1

CHAPTER 11

An Irrepressible Spirit

BRIEFING—SOUTH AFRICA

In 1948, the all-white Afrikaner National Party of South Africa introduced the policy of apartheid which called for the separation of the races. Bantu [black], colored [mixed race], and Asian no longer shared with whites the full rights of citizenship. Interracial marriages were banned. Many public institutions were restricted to whites only. "Pass" laws were enacted to limit the movement of nonwhites in white neighborhoods and effectively made them aliens in the land of their birth.

One of the many persons who grew up under apartheid is a dynamic lawyer who has dedicated his life to protecting the rights of children and to the restoration of full democracy to South Africa.

Peter Volmink

Lawyer-activist–South Africa

When I was a child my highest ambition was to pack shelves in a supermarket. My friends, who dropped out of school, had jobs packing shelves. With the few rands they earned, they bought jeans and shirts. I was very, very envious of that. I said to myself, "One day I'm going to be a shelf packer."

Everything in the lives of a person of color growing up in apartheid South Africa suggested that we couldn't even dream about being anything other than laborers, shelf packers, factory workers. The grand philosophy of apartheid destined us to be the hands and feet on factory floors that produced the wealth. The white folk were destined to be the bosses who ran the factories.

In our family of seven, I was second from the youngest. Our home was comparatively humble. My mom was a tea lady; she made tea for the white bosses in an oil company. My dad was a laborer for the local municipality of Cape Town. He dug holes and worked in the department of sewers. My dad didn't have much education, but he was involved in the community. He, a man of no education, chaired the parent-teachers' association, worked with the trade unions, and dealt with a range of social issues. My mom was also very strong. She got up very, very early, at about four A.M., to wake us in order to start studying. She'd make coffee and sandwiches and sit right beside us to make sure that we did our homework. My parents said, "Education is the only way out from where you are now."

Because of their efforts, each of my siblings is established in a profession.

The church and family are very important, especially in the political and cultural context that I come from. I couldn't have made it alone. There were so many things to draw us away from discovering what we could become as a people. Gangsters, for instance, were in abundance. As an eight-year-old kid, I vividly remember sitting on the street corner Saturday afternoons with my cousin Desmond, waiting for the gang fight. We would bet which gang was going to win the fight that inevitably happened. If it hadn't been for my family, I would have gone that way, too.

In apartheid South Africa, people of color could not vote for representatives in Parliament. We had to have a separate group of people to vote for, called the Colored Representative Council, the "Uncle Toms" of South Africa. In 1975, when I was fourteen years old, there was an election held in our community. The government sent their own handpicked stooges for us to vote for. It was a worthless vote.

We were young kids and we went out and said, "Look, these guys are stooges, we don't want them." It was a fun thing for us to do. We went out singing and dancing. While we were peacefully demonstrating, a truckload of policemen pulled up. They wore camouflage uniforms and carried batons. They had automatic weapons and dogs. The police charged at us. Some of us kids got beaten, others had dogs set on them. A number of kids got arrested. Luckily, nothing happened to me, but I left that place completely shocked. Up until that time, I had no idea how vicious this system could actually be. Because this event traumatized us kids so much, we became extremely

197

militant. If the apartheid guys had been smarter, they would not have treated kids that harshly. They created a generation of revolutionaries. That is what we became.

In South African apartheid, there were four separate societies: white, black, colored, and Asian (predominately Indian). These societies were deeply divided. Each group had to stick to its own little camp corner. Each had its own schools, communities, sporting facilities, and so on. There were separate education budgets for each of these groups. The education budget was extremely unequal. While white kids actually made up the minority of all the kids in South Africa, they walked away with the lion's share of the education budget. And that resulted in things like very few books in our schools, broken desks, unqualified teachers. We developed a term called "gutter education." We said that this education belongs in the gutter.

Opposition groups such as the African National Congress (ANC) and the United Democratic Front were established, only to be banned. Leaders of these parties were killed (Steve Biko), persecuted (Archbishop Tutu), or imprisoned (Nelson Mandela). The reaction to apartheid sparked many uprisings: Sharpville in 1960, Soweto in 1976, and the nationwide revolt during the 1980s.

Anti-apartheid reaction occurred in many countries during the sixties and seventies. International sanctions were extended to trade, finance, sports, and culture. A worldwide economic embargo isolated South Africa culturally and economically. But it also made it more confrontational.

Rebellion

In 1976, in solidarity with the Soweto uprisings, we began our own rebellion. The uprising wasn't a heavy political issue. We just wanted books in our school. There were no books. Once again, we took to the streets and sang a few songs. And once again, we got the same treatment—cops setting dogs on us, chasing us. But because we now had two years of militancy, we didn't take this lying down. Young as we were, we took to the streets and started to engage the police in battle. We threw stones and burned tires on the road to stop the trucks. It didn't stop them. They got through. And we were beaten.

Things got worse and worse from that point on. In 1980, a third uprising sent lots of our kids to prison. Some friends of mine went into exile to join the military wing of the ANC (African National Congress)—*Unkontho we Sizwe*, which means "The Spear of the Nation."

I was able to get ahead, not because of the system of education, but in spite of it. There were a number of obstacles. A university had been established for complacent, colored intellectuals who wouldn't question the government—at least that's how the government viewed it. It was called the University of the Western Cape. I didn't want to go there, although, let me say, the University of the Western Cape turned its given purpose completely on its head. It produced some of the most outstanding leaders of our struggle and became one of the most radical campuses in our country.

A person of color could not go to the white University of Cape Town without receiving prior permission from the government. A person of color could get permission only if there was a subject offered at the white university that was not offered at the colored people's university. I had to go and knock at the white man's door for permission, which was a very humiliating thing to do, especially given my frame of mind at the time. That was very hard. But I knocked and was accepted.

I studied law at the University of Cape Town with the help of a student loan that had to be paid back soon after I graduated. The only job that I could get to help pay back the loan was as a prosecutor. That was an interesting job for me to have in apartheid South Africa at that time.

About two days into the job, all hell broke loose when the police brought in their prisoners to be prosecuted. Some of them had their arms broken during interrogation sessions. Others had deep gashes on their faces and bodies. I adjourned the proceedings, released the prisoners, and prosecuted the policemen for assault. To say the least, the cops were completely upset by this. Here was a young black prosecutor charging senior white police officials with a crime. This wasn't the way it was supposed to work.

It all came to a head about two months later, when a truckload of black prisoners was brought in. Their sole crime was that they were in a white area without permission. I threw the case out of court. There was no way I was going to prosecute this. I got a call from "big brother" in Pretoria, the director of the Ministry of Justice, who asked me what the hell I was doing. I said that there was no way I could reconcile this law with my conscience. He gave me an ultimatum: "Either you prosecute them or get out!"

I had a very short career as a prosecutor in South Africa.

ELECTIONS?

In 1983, South Africa held some very funny elections. The government said, "Hang on, let's not have a separate parliament that colored people can vote for. Let's actually take the stooges that we elected earlier and make them members of Parliament." Now we were able to vote for people in Parliament, except it was a separate parliament. The white government was still up to its old tricks. Colored could vote for people in the colored parliament. Indians could vote for people in an Indian parliament. And whites could vote for people in a white parliament, which of course controlled everyone. And the blacks couldn't vote at all because of some very convoluted reasoning that they came from a separate homeland, hence they were not eligible to vote.

I got involved in another "don't vote" campaign. We could not legitimize this sham. Again, there was a lot of repression around that. The United Democratic Front, an alliance of nongovernmental organizations involved in the struggle against apartheid, was formed. Everything came to a head in 1985, when the government said, "We are under attack by revolutionaries and enemies of the state. The government has got the right to defend itself. The security of the state is being undermined by instigators and Communist sympathizers." We had heard this rhetoric for quite some time in the news and on the radio. We knew something was coming. Then the government declared a state of emergency.

The state of emergency was designed to crush the opposition. Severe restrictions were imposed on the re-

*porting of opposition news in the media. Between
1984 and 1993, more than 17,000 nonwhite South
Africans were killed and many more were injured or
imprisoned.*

The state of emergency in South Africa was seen to a large extent as a war against children. Children were at the forefront at the time of the uprising. High school kids and primary school kids in the remotest hamlets of South Africa participated. In the small towns that had been under the heel of repression, young kids were standing up and speaking out. Thousands of children got picked up and taken off to prison.

I remember very vividly coming home from work just after the state of emergency had been declared. While driving down Thornton Road in my neighborhood, I saw lots of people standing around. I inched up behind a police truck whose back doors were opened. There was a cop sitting with a rifle. I looked into this truck and I saw someone lying on the floor, but I couldn't make out who it was. The cop was saying, "Move away, don't follow us."

Here's what had happened: At the time the kids who were very militant stoned anything owned by the government. The government owned the railway company. Kids often threw stones at the railway company trucks. This time, at a given signal, cops jumped out from crates stacked inside the truck and opened fire on the kids. They were shot in cold blood. These kids were ten, eleven, twelve years old. This later became known as The Trojan Horse incident.

This event made the blood of the community boil. Though the kids were throwing stones at the railway truck, the sentence for that, even in apartheid South Africa, was not death. The cops were in essence being the judge, prosecutor, and executioner in a matter of seconds. There were a host of other incidents like that.

Kids between fourteen and seventeen were sent to jail for five to seven years. Out of school, into prison. In many cases they were tortured, humiliated, and brutalized. Many of them were burned as a result of the tortures by the security police. Electric probes would be attached to their fingers, toes, and genitalia. Police cuffed their hands and put bags over their heads which were then tied around their necks. Then buckets of water were poured over their heads so that they practically suffocated.

There were many accounts of kids being stripped naked . . . beaten . . . deprived of sleep . . . told that their parents had been killed. The parents had no right to see the kids once they were detained. Lawyers had no right to see the kids. Their priest or minister had no right to see them. The only people who had a right to visit them were the security police.

I had just started working in a law firm when the state of emergency began. I represented lots of kids, some of them as young as ten. They got arrested for committing crimes of public violence, which often meant just marching in the street.

During my stay with the firm, I handled quite a number of human rights cases, particularly with squatters. There were very, very vicious laws against squatters in South Africa, where police would come during the coldest nights in the winter and break up the squatters' camps. They would be left to huddle together in the cold and rain with all their belongings.

The definition of terrorism was so vague as to include anyone who caused an obstruction in road traffic. If I marched down the road and caused a traffic jam, I could be charged with terrorism and taken away to jail for a very long time.

We also had a notorious law called "the Suppression of Communism Act," which basically defined communism as anything opposed to government policy. Many South Africans were labeled Communist because of this.

Isaac Zenzile

One of my cases concerned a fifteen-year-old boy by the name of Isaac Zenzile. He was a young kid who lived in a rural town, Knysna, about 500 kilometers out of Cape Town. The year 1987 was a time of great unrest all over the country because there were lots of clashes between the youth and police, who, as agents of the apartheid regime, were seen as the enemy.

To prevent the police from coming into the township, a group of kids set up a barricade by burning tires across the road. The police came and removed the burning tires and the kids ran away. Soon after, the kids returned and resurrected the barricades. The police returned. This cat-and-mouse game went on for quite a while throughout the evening. Then the police came by again, removed the tires, and drove away. The kids heard someone shout, "Come back! Worthless dogs are gone." The kids came back not knowing that it was one of the policemen who shouted. There were about three to five policemen waiting in the bushes. When the kids came out, the cops jumped out and without prior warning opened fire with live ammunition. These kids were between thirteen and fourteen. One was killed instantly. My client, Isaac Zenzile, was partially crippled. The matter went to trial. I acted on his behalf to claim compensation from the state for what we regarded as an unlawful shooting of this young boy.

I visited the scene of the crime in preparation for the trial. Standing there, I projected myself back into the time when the shooting took place. I felt extremely angry, especially knowing that an act like this one had taken place hundreds, in fact, thousands of times.

What I found encouraging was my client's own sense of buoyancy, in spite of the shooting. When I spoke to him I didn't sense any bitterness at all. He laughed and talked about life in the townships and watching a soccer game. He was like any other young person.

It's a very odd thing to explain, but I think our people have an irrepressible spirit. Even in the most traumatic of circumstances, hope triumphs. I interpret that as a declaration that we are not going to be robbed of life. We are not going to be robbed of our humanity. We will continue to celebrate life even in a situation of shooting and killing. We refuse to give up the ability to laugh and to love and to live, despite an extremely oppressive situation.

Interestingly, the state decided to settle the case. They offered a sum of money to Zenzile's family. I spoke to my client and said that the amount that they offered was very minor, 50,000 rand [about $10,000 U.S.]. But my client came from a very poor rural community. He accepted the money.

The firm that I worked for was mainly a commercial firm. My work wasn't generating the kind of fees that they wanted. I represented squatters who could afford only twenty rand. That's about four U.S. dollars. One case became a two-day trial. I was in court from eight until four on both days. I took the case because I couldn't say to people who are in prison, "No, sorry, you only have four dollars."

STREET LAW

At the time, I felt that justice would be best served by informing everyday people about their fundamental legal rights. As a lawyer, I felt that I was not effective enough for the people I was serving. A friend and I started speaking out about democracy, a very foreign concept to us South Africans. We realized that democracy is not just a way of governing, it is a way ordinary people relate to each other. We launched a program to teach the law and to teach human rights principles nationwide throughout South Africa. We've taken human rights education into prisons, which have been notorious for their human rights violations. We've taken it onto farms in the remote areas of South Africa. We used all kinds of methods to get people excited: street theater, music, mock trials, art, and dance. We called it "edu-tainment."

I joined an organization called "Street Law," which is geared to teaching people their fundamental rights. I was asked to start up the Cape Town chapter. We produced a range of manuals about a person's rights when arrested, when questioned by the police, when assaulted by the police. We have taken this program to thousands of high schools all over South Africa. We also have a program for prisoners. It's all about prisoners' rights, which is actually an oxymoron.

Michelle Beard, an American lawyer who currently works for Human Rights Watch, came to South Africa and we put together the first-ever human rights camp. Sixty kids from a cross section of the country attended, including the niece of the minister of police. For three days, we lived in the mountains and introduced kids to the United Nations' Universal Declaration of Human Rights. A group of white attorneys lent their support to this program.

South Africa is full of ironies. Things aren't always clear cut. It isn't as if all the white folk are bad and all the black folk are good. There are many, many white people who have been outstanding human rights activists and there are many, many black people who have been notorious villains in the camp of apartheid.

Recently, I was working with a group of street actors on a play called *Know Your Rights When You Are Arrested*. While the play was in progress, we were arrested. By that time, I knew what to say and I advised other actors as well. When the police found out that I was an attorney, they backed down and released us. In retrospect it was actually rather funny.

In the early nineties, the government searched for new economic opportunities and an end to the international sanctions. F. W. de Klerk was elected president and the thirty-year ban on the ANC was lifted. Nelson Mandela, a leader in the African National Congress, was released from prison after serving twenty-seven years.

The National Party and the ANC agreed to participate in a government of national unity based on a power-sharing arrangement. The first national multiracial elections were held April 26–29, 1994, result-

ing in a resounding victory for the ANC. Nelson Mandela, the leader of the party, became the president of South Africa.

Nelson Mandela was released from prison and apartheid was finally, finally rescinded. Because of our children's experiences with the law, a number of them have been traumatized. Many have become completely alienated from society. They are uneducated. They have very bitter memories of torture, humiliation, and extreme harassment. These kids are called the "lost generation." I don't like the term because I don't think those kids are lost. But they are bitter and they are angry. We cannot turn a blind eye to them. We need to help these kids work through that anger. If we don't, this actually constitutes a serious new threat to human rights which will come back to haunt us.

THE RIGHT TO VOTE

As a black South African—and I consider myself black even though I am of mixed race—I had never voted in my life. I'd studied electoral laws. I knew all about the electoral systems throughout the world. I could tell you about proportional representation and winner-takes-all systems. But I myself had never voted. In April 1994, I cast my first ballot. It was such a moving experience for my wife Margaret and me to go into the voting booth with pens in hand to make the cross for the first time.

The day of the elections was incredible. We arrived at the election booth at about six o'clock in the morning, thinking that we would be first in line. When we arrived, a queue of people already stretched on for blocks. By nine in the morning there were queues going down about a mile or so. It was raining. The people stood firm. They said, "We have been waiting all our lives for this moment and are not going to turn around now because of a little rain." It was the most peaceful day in South Africa in a very, very long time.

A MESSAGE FROM PETER:

I believe that people are made for each other. We are made to look out for each other. We are made to support each other. We are made to struggle for each other through difficult times. I learned very valuable lessons as a kid—the importance of family and faith, the importance of community, the importance of people helping each other. I have had some achievements, educationally and professionally, but I didn't get here by myself. I'm standing on the shoulders of a whole host of people who made sure that I got where I am today. And hopefully, one day other people will stand on my shoulders.

Postscript

You are cordially invited to a celebration. . . .
Date: December 6, 1994
Place: The American Museum
  of Natural History, New York City
Event: Human Rights Watch Award Ceremony

Peter Volmink of South Africa approaches the steps of the stage at the American Museum of Natural History. Peter is one of nine activists from around the world who have come to New York to receive the Human Rights Watch Award. Accompanying Peter is his friend, Michelle India Beard, counsel to Children's Watch. Michelle will introduce Peter when the awards are given out.

During the ceremony that precedes a sell-out gala dinner party at the museum, representatives from the various divisions introduce each monitor. Two honorees are not present because their governments will not allow them to leave their countries. They are represented on the stage by empty chairs. The chairs are stunning reminders of the dangers that these monitors face every day.

Robert L. Bernstein, the chair of Human Rights Watch, and Kenneth Roth, the executive director, open the ceremony. Ken says, "We must demonstrate that through consistent public condemnation, tough and coordinated economic pressure, and a prospect that murderers and torturers will face trial and prison, even the most repulsive human rights abuses can be curbed.

"None of the work would be possible without the brave men and women with whom I'm honored to share the stage this evening. They and their colleagues around the world represent the front line of the human rights movement. Abusive governments everywhere try to hide their misdeeds behind closed doors. These human rights monitors try to pry the doors open to expose these crimes and subject their authors to the public scrutiny that compels change. It is a sad tribute to the power of their work that governments regularly target them and their colleagues. In the past year, twenty-four human rights monitors were murdered for their work. A terrible toll."

In spite of the sadness for those who are not present, in spite of the anger at the evil acts that force organizations such as this one to exist, this night is an evening of celebration. It is an evening of laughter. It is an evening of solidarity.

Irrepressible Spirit cannot end without an acknowledgment of the other monitors who shared the stage with Peter and Michelle.

Peter, Jean-Claude, Dimitrina, Monique, and Ken

Bao Tong—*China*

An empty chair, carrying the name "Bao Tong," is onstage while the man sits in a prison cell in China. He is accused of "leaking an important state secret" and of "counterrevolutionary propaganda and incitement."

Sidney Jones, executive director of Human Rights Watch/Asia, introduces the empty chair. She explains that Bao Tong is serving his fifth year of a seven-year sentence in a prison in Beijing. He is not a rebel or a dissident, but someone who had been working for economic and political reform within the Chinese political system. At the time of his arrest, Bao Tong was a senior Chinese official, director of the Chinese Communist Party's research center for the reform of the political structure.

Sidney says, "He was arrested because he was on the losing side of a domestic power struggle. The side he was on was a group of reformers who were not only sympathetic to the students in Tiananmen Square, but who also favored greater political and economic reform."

Accepting the award on behalf of Bao Tong is his son, Bao Pu. In the last five years, Bao Pu has been conducting a one-person campaign for the release of his father.

Bao Pu walks to the stage, smiles at the other honorees, kisses Sidney, and says, "Two weeks before my father's arrest, knowing of the impending danger, he handed my mother and me copies of different regulations and laws pertaining to the protection of an individual from arbitrary detention. He said, 'Realistically, these will not protect me. But at least you have a case. And remember, this is the way it should be done.'

"Five years later I visited the prison. Never had I been so devastated as to see him there. I told him, 'People still remember you.'

"He smiled gently and said, 'It doesn't matter if people remember me.'

"I want to make sure that history does not forget my father."

Moncef Marzouki—*Tunisia*

Moncef Marzouki is a doctor, a professor of medicine, and a prominent human rights monitor in Tunisia. In March 1994, he was arrested and imprisoned on charges relating to his promotion of rights to free expression and association. Although he was released in July, he still awaits trial.

Until the very last minute, Human Rights Watch had hoped Dr. Marzouki would be allowed to attend this event, but the government of Tunisia will not allow him to travel to the United States. When all hope failed, an empty chair with his name on it was placed on the stage.

Chris George, executive director of Human Rights Watch/Middle East, says, "We could fill the stage with empty chairs that represent human rights activists from the Middle East. But we wanted Dr. Marzouki. We wanted him to be here because he's from Tunisia, which portrays itself as a bastion of democracy and respect for human rights. Because he's from Tunisia, we expected him to be here. But we were wrong. Tunisia thinks that by keeping Dr. Marzouki in their country they can keep information from getting out. They are wrong. And we will prove them wrong. Inspired by Dr. Marzouki's courage, his tenacity, his creativity, we will work harder to support his efforts, and the efforts to promote and protect human rights in Tunisia and throughout the Middle East."

When Human Rights Watch was certain that Dr. Marzouki would not attend this ceremony, they contacted his daughter Myriam, who lives in Paris. Hours off the plane, she accepted the award on behalf of her father.

Myriam says, "I'm very proud to be here in the place of my father, but I would have preferred that he be here tonight. I spoke to him on the phone yesterday and he told me that his situation was becoming more and more pressured. He also asked me to thank Human Rights Watch for everything you have done to support human rights work in the past and more than ever now."

And those who came . . .

Jean-Claude Jean—*Haiti*

In 1992, Jean-Claude Jean helped form the Haitian Human Rights Platform, a national consortium of nine nongovernmental organizations. One of the Platform's activities is to make public information about abuses in Haiti. Jean-Claude also works directly with victims of abuse by getting them medical and legal assistance. In 1994, the Platform was forced to close its doors on several occasions because of death threats directed against its members. In August 1994, following the murder of his friend and colleague Father Jean-Marie Vincent, Jean-Claude was forced into hiding. He personally has received numerous death threats.

Jean-Claude's organization is currently working to establish a truth commission that will bring gross abusers of human rights to justice. He says, "When one realizes how long is the list of victims of people [in Haiti] who have disappeared and been murdered, one cannot help but think that the road to recovery is still very long. In order for this award not to be just a mere symbol, it creates a very great moral responsibility for the person who receives it and a very great duty of solidarity from those who give it. May everyone present tonight continue to encourage us to pursue the courageous struggle of the Haitian people to restore their dignity and protect the rights of freedom and life."

Deborah Labelle—*The United States*

The United States now has the highest population of prisoners of any country (for whom we have data).[1] As the population of women prisoners grows, problems arise concerning their well-

Alison, Deborah, Ricardo, Joseph, and I.A.

being and their children's well-being. For example, the separation of the children from the women has become an issue that needs to be addressed. In the mid-1980s, male guards were brought in to guard women prisoners. The number of rapes and assaults increased dramatically.

For the last nine years, Deborah Labelle, a civil rights attorney and advocate on behalf of women prisoners, has persistently challenged the Michigan Department of Corrections to provide equal and adequate services to women. Deborah warns that the easiest way to do away with human rights is first to deprive a group that has no way to be heard. She says that because prisoners have become a despised group, there are increasing violations of their human rights.

Deborah says, "I appreciate HRW's willingness to recognize

the existence of human rights violations in this country. I think that to look at such abuses at home gives us more credibility to address the violations elsewhere.

"I accept this award as an acknowledgment of the necessity of addressing the rights of prisoners and on behalf of all the activists in prison who struggle for dignity and a second chance."

Joseph Mudumbi—*Zaire*

Joseph Mudumbi is a lawyer from Goma, Zaire. His home is just across the lake from Rwanda. When he heard about the genocide there, he ran from his house into the streets to rescue people. He managed to save over sixty Rwandans. He then set up a kind of underground railroad to rescue more people from the killings in Rwanda.

Joseph is currently working to assure that the refugee population in his country is not held hostage by the extremist elements in the camps. He's also working with an international tribunal on war crimes to ensure that those guilty of genocide will be tried.

Joseph says, "When I was a young boy, I had been told that American people are always killing my people. But through my work I met American people: human rights activists, journalists, and humanitarian associates who came to my country in order to learn what had happened and to help. . . . I hope that the gift of communication will be opened with many contacts like this."

Father Ricardo Rezende—*Brazil*

Father Rezende is a parish priest ministering to the rural poor in Rio Maria, in the heart of the Brazilian Amazon. He has been an essential force in denouncing the practice of forced labor in Brazil, where poor laborers are enticed with false promises of high wages to work on distant ranches, and then forced to labor for months without rest. Although his name appears on a death list that has claimed the lives of five others, Father Rezende will not leave his people.

"I know that when you honor me you also honor those in my country who gave their lives for a better life in the rural areas."

Dimitrina Petrova—*Bulgaria*

Before the fall of communism, Dimitrina Petrova gave up her job as a professor of philosophy to work as a human rights activist in the dissident movement in Bulgaria. Afterward, she became the supervisor for the Bulgarian Human Rights Project and defended the region's most marginalized and least represented minority—the Romas (Gypsies). She is a field officer for the International Helsinki Federation for Human Rights.

In Bulgaria, Dimitrina started several projects, including citizens for religious tolerance, freedom of expression groups, and children at risk groups. Dimitrina says that the most challenging and difficult part of her work is with the Gypsies in Bulgaria. The second most challenging part of her work is everything in Albania.

Dimitrina says, "Two weeks ago the Bulgarian newspaper published an article entitled 'Bulgaria does not need foreign enemies as long as it has its domestic human rights monitors.' These are the words of an important governmental official. Of course, we will not hear this position expressed in an official statement. But it still remains a predominant stereotype in the thinking of the governments in today's Eastern Europe.

"This is why it is a matter of principle for the human rights organizations to support the vulnerable human rights community in Eastern Europe. I am profoundly happy to inhabit the same universe of concern and determination, despair and hope, with the people of Human Rights Watch."

I. A. Rehman—*Pakistan*

For over thirty years I. A. Rehman has been a political journalist and human rights activist. During the martial law period of 1980s, he was the associate editor of a weekly newspaper, *Viewpoint,* the only source of human rights information. For his writing and activism, he spent six months in prison and was forbidden to travel abroad for many years.

I. A. says, "We promise to be around for a long, long time. Stay by our sides. Together we have a job to do. We will transform the direction of human rights into a universal reality so that everybody, regardless of color, belief, or gender, will have the freedom to love and to smile."

Other Human Rights Organizations

Amnesty International USA
322 Eighth Avenue
New York, NY 10001
(212) 807-8400
A worldwide movement of people working for the release of all prisoners of conscience, for fair and prompt trials for all political prisoners, and for an end to torture and the death penalty.

Children's Defense Fund
25 E Street, NW
Washington, DC 20001
(202) 628-8787
Provides a voice for the children of America, who cannot vote, lobby, or speak out for themselves with particular attention to the needs of poor, minority, and disabled children.

Doctors Without Borders/Médecins Sans Frontières (MSF)
11 East 26 Street, Suite 1904
New York, NY 10010
Tel: (212) 679-6800
Fax: (212) 679-7016
The world's largest voluntary medical emergency relief organization.

It offers assistance to populations in distress, victims of natural or man-made disasters, and victims of armed conflicts. Every year Doctors Without Borders sends over 2,000 volunteer doctors, nurses, and logistics experts to more than 65 countries.

Global Kids
729 Seventh Ave.
New York, NY 10019
A global and multicultural education and leadership development organization that gives young people a voice on issues of importance to them.

The Lawyers Committee for Human Rights
330 Seventh Ave.
New York, NY 10001
tel: (212) 629-6170
fax: (212) 967-0916
e-mail: NYC@Ichr.org
    Washington, D.C., office:
    100 Maryland Avenue, NE
    Suite 502
    Washington, DC 20002
    tel: (202) 547-5692
    fax: (202) 543-5999
    e-mail: WDC@Ichr.org
Works to protect and promote fundamental human rights. Its work is impartial, holding all governments to the standards affirmed in the international Bill of Human Rights. The Lawyers Committee has a particular interest in building legal systems and structures that will provide stable, long-term guarantees for human rights at the national and international levels, and in building close and active partnerships with nongovernmental human rights advocates around the world.

National Gay and Lesbian Task Force
1734 14 Street, NW
Washington, DC 20009
(202) 332-6483
Membership organization advocating the civil rights of gays and les-

bians that uses lobbying, grassroots organizing, public education, and direct action.

National Organization for Women (NOW)
1000 16 Street, NW, Suite 700
Washington, DC 20036-5705
(202) 331-0066
Organization dedicated to bringing women into full participation in the mainstream of American society.

National Street Law Programme
P.O. Box 18658
Wynberg, Cape Town 7824
South Africa
Tel: (021) 797-6158
Fax: (021) 797-8306
Imparts elementary legal and human rights knowledge to school children and disadvantaged communities.

Oxfam America
115 Broadway
Boston, MA 02116
(617) 482-1211
An international agency funding self-help and disaster relief in poor countries in Africa, Asia, Latin America, and the Caribbean and distributing educational materials for people in the United States on issues of development and hunger.

Reebok Human Rights Award
Reebok International, Ltd.
100 Technology Center Drive
Stoughton, MA 02072
tel: (617) 341-5000
fax: (617) 297-4806
Seeks to honor individuals thirty years of age or under from around the world who have made significant contributions to the cause of human rights, often against great odds.

End Notes

CHAPTER THREE

1. HRW/Helsinki, *War Crimes in Bosnia-Hercegovina* (New York: Human Rights Watch, 1992), p. 30.

2. Ibid., p. 19.

3. HRW/Helsinki, *War Crimes in Bosnia-Hercegovina, Volume II* (New York: Human Rights Watch, 1993), p. 18.

4. Ibid., pp. 103–4.

5. Ibid., p. 21.

6. Ibid., pp. 216–18.

7. Ibid., p. 175.

CHAPTER FIVE

1. See HRW/Americas, *Final Justice: Police and Death Squad Homicides of Adolescents in Brazil* (New York: Human Rights Watch, 1994), pp. viii–ix.

2. Ibid., p. 82.

CHAPTER SIX

1. Steve Jones, "The Perfect Electric Chair? Send for Mr. Edison," *Daily Telegraph,* 8 February 1995; John G. Leyden, "Death in the Hot Seat: A Century of Electrocutions," *Washington Post,* 5 August 1990.

2. Human Rights Watch, American Civil Liberties Union, *Human Rights Violations in the United States* (New York, Human Rights Watch 1993), p. 130.

3. *McCleskey v. Kemp,* 481 U.S. 279, 286–87 (1987).

4. *Darden v. Wainwright,* 477 U.S. 168 (1986).

CHAPTER SEVEN

1. Asia Watch/Women's Rights Project, *A Modern Form of Slavery: Trafficking of Burmese Women and Girls into Brothels in Thailand* (New York: Human Rights Watch, 1993), pp. 38–39.

2. Ibid., p. 3.

3. HRW/Asia, *Rape for Profit: Trafficking of Nepali Girls and Women to India's Brothels* (New York: Human Rights Watch, 1995), p. 19.

4. Ibid., pp. 34–35.

CHAPTER TEN

1. See HRW/Helsinki, "Return to Tajikistan," *A Human Rights Watch Short Report,* vol. 17, no. 9, May 1995, pp. 3–9.

2. HRW/Helsinki, "Tajik Presidential Election Conducted in Climate of Fear and Fraud," *A Human Rights Watch Press Release,* November 9, 1994.

3. Grolier's Academic American Encyclopedia, *Online edition,* Grolier Electronic Publishing, 1994.

POSTSCRIPT

1. Fox Butterfield, "Idle Hands Within the Devil's Own Playground," *New York Times,* 16 July 1995. There are now 1.5 million inmates in

state and federal prisons and city and country jails around the nation, more than triple the number in 1970, and they are serving longer sentences; Marc Mauer, "Americans Behind Bars: The International Use of Incarceration, 1992–93," *The Sentencing Project,* September 1994.

Selected Bibliography

I have read a number of books about human rights that are extremely moving. Here are a few that I would like to share with you.

Arendt, Hannah. *Eichmann in Jerusalem*. New York: Penguin Books, 1977.

Arendt, Hannah. *The Origins of Totalitarianism*. 2nd Edition. New York: Meridian Books, 1958.

Frankel, Marvin E. (with Ellen Saidman). *Out of the Shadows of the Night: The Struggle for International Human Rights*. New York: Delacorte Press, 1989.

Ingle, Joseph B. *Last Rights: Thirteen Fatal Encounters with the State's Justice*. Nashville, Tennessee: Abingdon Press, 1990.

Levine, Ellen. *A Fence Away from Freedom: Japanese Americans and World War II*. New York: G.P. Putnam's Sons, 1995.

Li Lu. *Moving the Mountain*. London: Macmillan Books, 1990.

Prejean, Helen. *Dead Man Walking*. New York: Vintage Books, 1993.

Rezende, Ricardo. *Rio Maria: Song of the Earth*. Translated by Madeleine Adriance. New York: Orbis Books, 1994.

Temple, Frances. *A Taste of Salt: A Story of Modern Haiti*. New York: A Richard Jackson Book, Orchard Books, 1990.

Walls, David. *Activist's Almanac*. New York: Simon & Schuster, 1993.

If you are interested in learning more about specific human rights issues, Human Rights Watch has an annual subscription to all the publications issued by their regional divisions or projects. Individual reports and newsletters are also available to the public. Their informative catalog listing their publications is available by writing to:

Human Rights Watch
Publications Department
485 Fifth Avenue
New York, NY 10017-6104